COWBOY PROTECTOR

MARGARET DALEY

Published by Steeple Hill Books™

Special thanks and acknowledgment to Margaret Daley for her contribution to the PROTECTING THE WITNESSES miniseries.

STEEPLE HILL BOOKS

Recycling programs for this product may not exist in your area.

ISBN-13: 978-0-373-44385-7

COWBOY PROTECTOR

This edition published by arrangement with Steeple Hill Books.

www.SteepleHill.com

Printed in U.S.A.

God is our refuge and strength,
a very present help in trouble.
—*Psalms* 46:1

To Marta Perry, Debby Giusti, Shirlee McCoy,
Barbara Phinney and Lenora Worth—my comrades
in this Love Inspired Suspense continuity series.

PROLOGUE

Memo: Top Secret

To: FBI Organized Crime Division; U.S. Marshal's Office

From: Jackson McGraw, Special Agent, Chicago Field Office
Federal Bureau of Investigation

Date: Feb. 24, 2010

Re: Operation Black Veil

Another woman in Montana in the Witness Protection Program has been murdered. Although innocent of having any connection with the Martino crime family, her description is similar to Olivia Jensen's, the main witness in the upcoming trial of Vincent Martino. Steps are being made to tighten the security around Mrs. Jensen.

U.S. Marshals are searching for Jen Davis, a witness who disappeared two years ago, to warn her about the latest developments with female witnesses in her age range with green eyes and to bring her back into the program, if possible.

Marshals have a lead on her whereabouts and are in the process of locating her.

It has been confirmed there are two female targets the Martino crime family is interested in and will pursue to their deaths, Olivia Jensen and Eloise Hill. Contact SA McGraw with any information that will assist the FBI in its case against the Martino crime family.

ONE

Hannah Williams scanned the bus depot at Sweet Creek, Montana, tugging her heavy overcoat closer to her to ward off the chill of the biting wind that swooped down from the snow-capped mountains nearby. When her gaze paused on a stranger, she memorized the face, then moved on to the next one. She'd learned to be totally aware of the people and terrain surrounding her. Her life depended on it.

On her second sweep of the terminal, Hannah spied a newcomer who towered over the others around him. Wearing a black cowboy hat that blended with his black, straight hair and a camel-colored, sheepskin coat, he surveyed the crowd with dark coffee-colored eyes, his strong jaw set in a look of concentration. His tanned features were in stark contrast to most of the people in the depot who were pasty white from hibernating during the winter months. His command of his space touched off an alarm in her. Friend or foe? For a second she poised herself to run in case he wasn't the man she was to meet.

His intense gaze zeroed in on her. She stiffened and clutched her purse against her as though that would protect her from a bullet.

Run. Find another job, screamed through her mind.

I need the work. A ranch would be a perfect place to hide.

He headed for her, the throng parting to allow him through. With each stride that brought him closer, her heart increased its pounding. She took a step back.

Nearing her, he smiled, straight white teeth standing out against the bronze face, but all she could focus on was the cleft in his chin. Another man she knew had one. Its sight instantly threw her back into the past.

Devon Madison brushed up against her as she left the courthouse. The hatred spewing from him held her immobile. He leaned close and whispered, "I'm coming after you," in such a chilling, cultured voice she shuddered despite the summer heat radiating off the asphalt in Los Angeles.

She forced the memory back into its box, hopefully never to be opened again.

"Are you Hannah Williams?"

The question from the cowboy in front of her whisked her totally back to the present. *No, I'm Jen Davis.* But not anymore. She was reminded each time she heard a different name from the one given to her at birth. "Yes."

"I'm Austin Taylor. Pleased to meet you." His grin widened, two dimples appearing on either side of his mouth.

When he held out his hand, she shook it, a strong clasp with roughened fingers that fit the man before her.

"Let's get out of here. We have about a thirty-minute drive to the ranch." He gestured toward the parking lot. "My Jeep is this way."

She followed him to a dirt-covered, red SUV and slipped into the front passenger seat. "I'll need to catch the five-o'clock bus for Billings. Will that be a problem?"

"No. We can talk on the drive. Then when we reach the Triple T, you can meet my daughter, Misty, and spend some time with her."

"Great."

The town of Sweet Creek disappeared quickly as Austin headed west. After placing her purse on the floor by her feet, Hannah leaned back against the cushion and peered at the side mirror nearest her. Not any cars behind them. Good. Relaxation eased through her as she angled toward her prospective employer.

He glanced at her. "The person I hire for this job must have a good rapport with Misty. My daughter has been through a lot lately, and her usual cheerful disposition has suffered."

"You told me on the phone that she was in a car wreck four weeks ago. What are her medical concerns?"

"A broken leg with a cast that goes up to her thigh, a broken wrist and respiratory complications from the air bag deploying. I brought her home yesterday and will need someone to start within a few days. Misty has developed asthma and is having trouble with her breathing, not to mention the fact that it's hard for a child who was very active before the accident to be immobile. As you'll see my ranch is isolated. I need someone to be a companion and help with any medical issues that arise while I'm working. Later when her casts come off, Misty will have physical therapy exercises to do. I need someone who can follow the instructions given by the physical therapist."

"When are the casts coming off?" She didn't like staying any longer than two, maybe three months in one place.

"The doctor hopes to take the arm cast off in a few

weeks and see if he can remove the other one and put her in a leg immobilizer. But even then she won't be able to bear weight for a while."

"I've worked with patients who need to do certain exercises. That shouldn't be a problem at all."

He shot her another assessing gaze. "I'm thankful my grandmother knew of a good friend in Billings who's using home health care."

"I'm glad she got in touch with Mr. Peterson. My job with him is winding down. I was starting to look for another one, so this will work out perfectly. That is, if you hire me."

"Will you be able to start within three days? I got the impression from Granny that Saul was doing much better now."

Hannah glanced behind her, saw a white pickup a hundred yards back and tensed, her fingernails digging into her palms. Dragging her attention back to Austin, she uncurled her hands and forced a calmness into her voice that she never felt in an unfamiliar environment. *No big deal. Trucks are everywhere in Montana.* "Yes, Saul's doing very well." She pasted a grin on her face. "To tell you the truth, I could have left a couple of weeks ago, but I think he gets lonely and enjoys the company."

"He only had glowing words to say about you and your work. When Granny got off the phone, she was ready to hire you on the spot, sight unseen."

But you weren't, hence the invitation to come to the ranch for an interview and to meet your daughter. "I do have another reference if you need it." At least on the job before Saul Peterson's, she'd still gone by the name Hannah Williams. Soon she would change her name again—some variation of Williams or maybe it was time to pretend Williams had been a married name and she was now using her maiden name. She didn't want to get too comfortable in the same routine.

"Yeah, that's fine."

Hannah reached into her oversized purse and withdrew the manila envelope, then placed it on the seat between them. "Also in there is my resume with my medical training information."

He peered down at the envelope she laid on the seat between them. "Not only do I need someone who can administer Misty's medications and tend to her medically, as I said earlier, I need a companion to help take my daughter's mind off what has happened. According to Saul, you're quite entertaining. But he's seventy-six. How do you do with five-year-olds?"

"I love children and have worked with several over the past few years." *And each child has only confirmed my desire to have a family, something that's unattainable.*

"So you've worked in Billings. Where else?"

"All over Montana. Before Billings, I was in Great Falls, Missoula, Silver Gorge and White Bend, to name a few."

His eyebrows rose. "You do move around a lot. I can't imagine being away from my ranch for too long."

"Montana is beautiful, and I've been to some gorgeous places. I have no ties so I can move freely. Some places are remote and don't have access easily to home health care. I fill a need."

"No family?"

Hannah didn't have a family. Jen Davis did, but that person was dead to the world. She "died" five years ago, and Hannah had to remember that. Any slip could be fatal. "No family."

"Speaking of family, my grandmother Caroline, the one who knows Saul, lives with us. She's usually full of energy, but her diabetes is acting up. She wanted to take care of Misty by herself, but that would be too much for her. I want the person who works with my daughter to keep an eye on my grandmother, too. I'm afraid she isn't taking her medicine like she should. So much of our life has been disrupted with the accident."

"I also love working with older people. They always have such interesting lives. Why, Saul had been with the rodeo in his younger days, and I got to hear all about how to ride a bull and bronco. Enough to know I don't want to."

Austin chuckled. "Neither do I. I've spent more time on the ground than I care, breaking horses."

Hannah peered behind the Jeep and still saw the pickup hanging back about a hundred yards. The tension she'd managed to hold at bay while talking about the job instantly swamped her. When Austin turned off the highway onto a narrow paved road, the white truck mimicked his move. She clutched her hands together, her back ramrod straight to the point it ached.

"Relax. We're almost there."

Not five minutes later Austin turned off the road onto a gravel one, driving his Jeep under an arch proclaiming to the world they were on Triple T land. And the pickup trailed them.

Every couple of minutes Hannah threw a glance over her shoulder, trying to draw a decent breath. The truck was still behind them. She compelled air into her oxygen-deprived lungs.

"Do you realize someone is following us?" she finally asked as the SUV headed up a rise in the road.

"Yeah, that's my foreman. He'd gone to town for some supplies."

"Oh." Hannah sagged against the seat, her stress deflating like a balloon being pricked with a pin. She caught his evaluating gaze and cocked a grin. "I just thought it was unusual for someone else to turn off the highway then the road back there." As usual, she overreacted and needed to work on that. She was safe and nothing remotely dangerous had happened to her since she'd left the Witness Protection Program two years before. Not even the U.S. Marshal's office in Montana knew where she was, so how was Devon Madison going to find her?

"I employ nine people year-round. I've been hiring lately since this is the beginning of our busiest time of year. Some of my employees live on the ranch, some don't."

So new people would be arriving at the Triple T. She filed that bit of information away in case she got the job. She would need to keep track of them but not overreact when she saw someone new about the ranch. Searching the landscape, littered with horses on one side of the road and cattle on the other, she realized the Triple T was a huge operation.

The Jeep crested another rise and before Hannah stretched acres of land with a large two-story log home nestled among tall pines and firs. A deck skirted the length on two sides, and banks of floor-to-ceiling windows afforded a gorgeous view of the mountains and pastures cocooning the house. A curl of smoke from the chimney snaked upward toward the clouds.

As Hannah took in her surroundings, tranquility settled over her. A place she could find peace. If only that were possible. Maybe here she could finally stop being paranoid and enjoy the beauty, at least for a short time.

Austin pulled up to the front of his home under a wooden overhang that protected visitors from the elements. Hannah glanced back at the now-paved road and noticed the pickup continue on toward a barn set off about three hundred yards from the house. A corral with several horses in it flanked the structure's left side while what must be a bunkhouse was on the right with a pen containing a huge, black bull.

As Hannah exited the SUV, a gust of wind blew through the carport, catching her long hair. Strands whipped across her face. She hooked them behind her ears and hurried toward the double wooden and beveled glass doors. One opened, and a small woman in her late seventies supported by a cane stood, her white hair cut short in a pixie. Her bright, dark brown gaze lit when it connected with Hannah's.

"Goodness. It's cold out here. I don't think winter has left us yet." The woman stepped to the side to allow Hannah to enter the warm house, then waved her hand toward the room to the right. "I have a fire going in here." She plodded toward what looked like a living room through the opening off the large foyer.

Straight ahead a staircase led up to the second floor with a balcony and wooden railing overlooking the ground level. To the left Hannah peeked inside the dining room and saw a dark walnut table for twelve and two large crystal chandeliers hanging over it. The formality contrasted with the living area that Hannah finally turned toward and followed Austin into.

"This is my grandmother, Caroline Taylor. Granny, this is Hannah Williams." He indicated Hannah take a seat next to her on the brown leather sofa. Slipping into a chair across from both women, he opened the manila envelope and perused the papers Hannah had included. His gaze collided with hers, held it for a few seconds before he said, "We had a nice chat in the car." He swung his attention to Caroline Taylor. "Do you have any questions for Hannah?"

"Only one. Will you tell me about the children you've worked with? Saul mentioned you loved children."

"Yes, there was a little boy who lived next to Saul's and he loved visiting him. I started bringing extra goodies I made for the child and, of course, Saul, who has a sweet tooth." Hannah went on and described a few children she'd cared for. By the time she'd finished, she'd relaxed back, leaning against one arm of the sofa.

"So you've worked with someone as young as Misty?"

"My second client was six. I was with her two months. I hated leaving but was so glad she was better."

"I expect Misty to have a full recovery." Austin slid her papers back into the envelope. "Although her casts will come off soon, her ankle was shattered by the accident and she broke another bone in her leg. It'll be a while before she's running around and playing like she's used to. Right now she has a motorized wheelchair, and you better look out when she wants to go somewhere."

"May I meet her?" Hannah looked from him to his grandmother.

"She was resting, but she should be up by now. We moved her bedroom downstairs next to mine since she's in a wheelchair. There's another one on the other side of Misty where you could sleep, and there are two empty ones upstairs where Austin sleeps."

"I'll take Hannah to Misty's room." Austin rose in one fluid motion.

Hannah followed him from the room, trying not to

stare too much at his broad back. Even hidden beneath a white button-down, long sleeve shirt, she could see his muscular biceps. She got the feeling he was very involved in the running of his ranch. His large hands were work roughened, and as he'd driven down his gravel road, his gaze swept the terrain as though he were checking everything out, assessing what was going on. She'd learned to do the same thing but for different reasons. That skill had kept her alive.

He tapped lightly on a door then eased it open, peering inside.

"Is she here, Daddy?"

"See for yourself, munchkin." He entered, stepping to the side so his daughter could glimpse her.

Hannah grinned and came into the room. "I'm Hannah, Misty. I hear you've been a brave little girl." Crossing to the bed, she took the chair next to it.

Misty sat up, leaning back against the pillows, a pink satiny comforter pulled up over her hips. "Has Daddy showed you the horses?"

"I've seen some in the fields, but I haven't seen any up close. Do you ride?"

The five-year-old nodded, strands of her long, black hair falling forward over her shoulders. "I have a horse of my very own." Her mouth turned down in a pout. "I can't ride now."

Hannah slid a glance toward Austin, not sure what to say to that comment.

"You will when you get better." He clasped the bedpost that supported the canopy. "Candy is waiting for you. I'm taking special care of her until you can."

Misty's warm milk-chocolate eyes lit at the mention of Candy. "I want to see her. I miss her."

"I'll arrange something later today. Maybe bring Candy up to the house and let you show Ms. Williams."

"Oh, please call me Hannah." She swiveled her attention back to the little girl. "And you, too, Misty." Hannah was so much easier for her to remember to respond to than Ms. Williams. One of the toughest things she'd had to do was not to forget her new name, which was difficult since it was changing in some way about every six months. "I don't stand on formality." She looked again at Austin.

"We don't here, either. Do we, munchkin?"

"What's for-ma-now-tee?"

"Remember a few months back when we went to Grandma Kline's house and had dinner with all those fancy dishes and white lace tablecloth. That's formality."

"Oh. I couldn't talk at the table."

Austin frowned. "Well, Grandma Kline likes things done a certain way. She never believed children should speak till spoken to." He moved to Misty and ruffled her hair, then kissed her on the forehead. "You don't have to worry about that here. I'll leave you two to get to know each other." Then to Hannah, he said, "When you're through, come to my office at the back of the house."

"Will do." Hannah scooted her chair up to the bed while he left the room. "Tell me about Candy. Why did you name her that?"

Misty bent toward her, cupping her hands at the sides of her mouth as if to impart a secret. "I love candy. I love horses."

"That makes sense. I love candy, too. Maybe too much." She patted her stomach.

"I ate too much once and got sick. Daddy told me too much of a good thing can be bad for me."

"Yeah, he's right."

Misty's pout returned. "I haven't seen Candy in a long time. Daddy says she misses me. But I miss her more."

Like I miss my mother and little brother. All Hannah wanted to do was hug them again. She'd never let them go. She could still remember the fight her brother and she had gotten into the day before everything in her life had changed. She'd never really apologized and told him she was sorry, not face-to-face. A letter wasn't the same thing.

Misty hung her head and twisted her hands together. "I miss Mommy, too. She's with Jesus now."

Hannah laid her palm against the little girl's arm with the cast up to just below her elbow. "Honey, of course you do."

Misty sniffled and knuckled her tears away. "I shouldn't cry."

"It's okay when you're sad."

The little girl looked right at her with huge brown eyes, a glistening shine in them. "It makes Daddy sad when I do."

Hannah's heart cracked at the pain she heard in the child's quavering voice. She leaned close to Misty as though telling her a secret. "I won't tell if you cry when I'm with you."

The little girl's forehead crinkled, and a baffled expression entered her eyes. "You wouldn't tell?"

"Nope. Sometimes girls just need a good cry. Men don't always understand that." She wished she had someone who would understand her tears. Someone she could explain the constant fear she lived with. But most people would never understand. Her life was the result of a split-second decision that had wiped everything she was familiar with away.

* * *

Austin stood at his large picture window in his office staring at the meadow where some of his horses grazed. He closed his eyes and a picture of Hannah Williams appeared—green eyes like two pieces of crystal, a sparkle in their depths, long, wavy hair the color of cinnamon and delicate features shaped into a beautiful countenance. The kind of beauty that screamed at him to run as fast as he could away from the woman. His deceased wife had that kind of beauty, and her restless spirit had driven her to lengths he'd never imagined when he'd married her.

When he glimpsed one of the mares teasing a stallion even with two fences and a road between them, he knew he wouldn't hire Hannah, although Saul sang her praises. Pivoting away from the window, he kneaded the tight cords of his neck. Ms. Hannah Williams was hiding something. He felt it deep in his gut, a warning he wished he'd had before marrying Jillian. A bitter taste coated his tongue. His wife's deceit destroyed any desire to leave himself open to that kind of betrayal. All he wanted to do was bury himself in his work and concentrate on Misty getting better.

The sound of his grandmother's cane on the hall's hardwood floor alerted him to her approach. He wiped his expression clear. Everything that had happened to Misty had exacted a toll on Granny, too.

She came into his office, a smile on her face. "I hope you hire Hannah."

"I know Saul recommended her, but I think I'll pass on her. We need someone who is older."

"I would want her even if Saul hadn't been the one to recommend her. I was going to escort her here to talk to you, but I didn't want to interrupt her conversation with

Misty. I heard your daughter actually laugh at something Hannah said. Did you hear me? Misty laughed. I haven't heard that sound in ages. I want that back in this house."

So do I. But if he hired Hannah, he'd go against his better judgment. "I don't know, Granny. I think she's hiding something."

"Check out her other reference. But I've got a feeling about Hannah that has nothing to do with what my friend said about her. She'd be perfect for Misty. That child needs her."

"Still…"

"All of us have something to hide from others. Can you honestly say you're totally above board with everyone you meet, especially the first time?"

"Well, no." He cracked a grin. "I at least wait till the second meeting before giving them my whole life history."

His grandmother flipped her wrist, her palm up. "There. That's my point. I'll keep an eye on her, but you know I'm rarely wrong about a person and I trust Saul's opinion. The Lord has sent her to us. I know it in here." She tapped her chest over her heart.

"I'll pray about it and check her other reference before I make my final decision."

"That's all I ask, Austin. I'll go get her. Try not to scare her off."

"I'll keep my growl to a purr."

As his grandmother left the office, Austin twisted back to the picture window. A snowflake cascaded down to the ground. Here it was the end of February and winter still had its grip on them, probably would for at least another month or longer. This was a busy time at the ranch with the births of the calves and foals. He still had a few more people to hire for the spring and summer. He didn't want to worry about who was taking care of his daughter.

Lord, if the other reference gives Hannah a glowing one then I'll hire her. But if it's less than glowing, I'll take that as a sign from You to find someone else.

A sound—a soft rap on wood—caught his attention, and he rotated toward it. His quick movement caused Hannah to step back, her body to tense, her eyes to widen. For a second fear flashed across her expression before she schooled it into a neutral one, the tension in her body melting away. His gut constricted as he sat and waved for her to have a seat in front of him.

"Hannah, is there anything in your past I should be aware of?"

TWO

Scrabbling for a safe answer to his loaded question, Hannah swallowed hard but kept her gaze trained on Austin, sitting behind his desk in his office. She wished she could share her past with someone because there were days the pain of loss beat her down, but that would be a foolish, dangerous move on her part. “No. I love what I do. My job is important to me.” Helping others was what kept her going on those days when thoughts of her past threatened to overwhelm her.

He nodded. “Do you have any questions about the job? About Misty?”

“She’s adorable, and I think I can help her.” The child was hurting physically, and emotionally, too. Although her mom was still alive, Hannah could identify with losing a mother.

“Then I’ll have an answer soon for you.” He stood, snatching up his set of keys. “A storm is moving in, and I want to make sure I get you back in time for your bus.”

Pushing to her feet, she started to tell him she could stay another hour and still get back before the bus to Billings left. She would like to spend some more time with Misty, but she was being dismissed. When she got back to Billings, she needed to look seriously for another job.

* * *

Later that night when Hannah finally fell into bed, sleep came quickly but so did the dream. Back in her rental house as if two years hadn't happened, Hannah heard the crashing sound of glass breaking. The noise of footsteps.

They've found me!

The words screamed through Hannah's mind, wrenching her from the nightmare that gripped her. Her eyes flew open, her limbs all tangled in something confining. Her thoughts jumbled, she fought for release. Frantic, she rolled, trying to get away.

The breath-jarring impact with her bedroom carpet totally woke her up. Her sheet held her prisoner in its snarled mess. Lying next to her bed, she shifted until she faced the ceiling and saw the lights from outside her apartment dancing on its spackled surface.

Drawing in deep gulps of air to calm her racing heartbeat, she tried to reassure herself that her nightmare hadn't been real—at least not the part about her being tackled by some unknown assailant. But the break-in two years ago had been very real. Real enough for her to flee the town where the Witness Protection Program had settled her, and when her time to report in with the U.S. Marshals had come last year, she'd let it pass without calling. She didn't know if the break-in had anything to do with her being in the program or not. She hadn't waited around to discover the truth because if it had been connected she would be dead by now.

She pushed herself up to a sitting position. Slowly the thundering of her heart eased. But as she scanned the dark recesses of her room, she could imagine some henchman lurking in one of them, waiting to pounce. A shiver chilled her. She dragged the tangled sheet about her shoulders and huddled under its warmth, wishing she didn't have such a vivid imagination.

She didn't have this nightmare much except when she planned to move to another location and for maybe the first week in the new place. But the trip yesterday to Bitterroot Valley and the Triple T Ranch had stirred up all her fears. Once she was settled she'd be okay—that was if Austin Taylor decided to hire her.

She had her doubts after the last meeting in his office and the silent trip back to Sweet Creek and the bus depot.

When he'd asked her if she had anything to hide, she'd hated lying to him, but how was she supposed to tell him that she had some evil people after her who would love to know where she was? Thankfully the nearly two years she'd been on her own without the Witness Protection Program, Devon Madison's goons hadn't found her because she was very careful. Staying in one place for three years could have possibly led someone to her front door. The key was constantly moving every few months, changing her name a couple of times, using cash and not leaving a paper trail in any name.

Finally rising, she shed her sheet and donned her lime-green terry-cloth robe. She needed coffee then a shower. She still had a job at Saul Peterson's. He'd told her to stay until she found another one. But she couldn't stay too long even if she didn't get a job right away. She had some money saved, if need be.

After fixing a pot of coffee and pouring a mug full, she parted the drapes in her living room overlooking the street in front of her apartment building. Only a few inches, but enough she could check out the area. She often found herself doing this when she was home, a habit she'd picked up early in the Witness Protection Program. One she wasn't going to give up even if she felt secure in her new identity.

She usually peered up and down the road, searching for any car parked that didn't belong. When she discovered one, she would note its tag number, description and keep tabs on it. She'd moved once in the middle of the night when a vehicle kept appearing out in front of her place. Discreet questions with her neighbors had left her puzzled with who was the owner of the Chevy. Later, she'd discovered quite by accident it was a man having a secret affair with a neighbor. That incident had reinforced her need not to panic, to use a clear-thinking judgment. Panic could lead to a mistake and, according to the man who'd helped her with her new identity in the beginning, could get her killed.

A sigh escaped her parted lips when she saw an empty street, except for a truck that traveled toward the east. The sky brightened to a rosy hue, splashing an array of colors from a pale baby blue to a lemon yellow. Time to get ready for work.

Taking several sips of her coffee, she surveyed the road one last time. A black Ford SUV drove around the corner and onto her street. It slowed and pulled into a spot across from her building. No one got out. She stepped back and farther to the side, then inched the curtains apart.

When ten minutes passed, she started to reach for her pad to write down the tag number, but a young woman came jogging down the sidewalk from the apartments across the street and slid into the passenger side of the SUV. It sped away.

Hannah collapsed against the back of the chair behind her, still clasping her mug between her hands. Would this constant fear ever go away? Probably not.

In her mind she truly believed that she was safe, but in her heart she couldn't quite shake her gut reaction to different situations—like an unknown vehicle on her street. She had to continue to work on that, or she would never have any kind of life. Any kind of peace.

Hannah got off the bus in front of Mama's Diner and hurried inside. She headed to a booth in the back near an exit and slipped onto the black vinyl cushion, worn in spots. Being a little late, she noticed the morning crowd was thinning. Her usual waitress gave her a smile, finished pouring some coffee for one of her customers, and then threaded her way through the maze of tables to Hannah.

"I thought maybe you'd taken a new job and had left Billings," Olivia Jarrod said as she set a mug on the table and filled it.

"I wouldn't leave without saying goodbye." Olivia was the closest person to a friend she'd had in a long, long time. From the beginning two months ago when Hannah had come into the diner for breakfast before going to Saul Peterson's around the corner, they had hit it off. It had been Olivia's first day on the job, and she'd been nervous, making a lot of mistakes. A few customers hadn't had much patience, but Hannah saw a person in need of a kind word. From that point on, she'd always sat in Olivia's area, and her friend had sometimes been able to join her for a cup of coffee if the crowd wasn't large. She'd miss Olivia. There was a connection with Olivia she couldn't explain.

Her hands still cold from a north wind bringing frigid weather, Hannah wrapped them around the navy-blue ceramic cup. "Ah, this feels good. It's cold out there."

"Yeah, I've felt it every time the door has opened." Her

friend looked around. "I'm due a break. I'll join you for a few minutes while you eat. Your usual?"

"Of course. I hate change and what I eat for breakfast I can control." So little else was totally in her control.

"Be back in a minute then."

As Olivia made her way to the counter, she stopped and gave her last customer his check, then she proceeded to the kitchen. Her long brown hair was pulled back in a ponytail while her blue eyes always held a touch of regret. That look of vulnerability spoke to Hannah on a level that prompted her to tell Olivia her story. She couldn't, of course, but the words had been on the tip of her tongue several times in the past couple of weeks when she realized she would have to move on soon.

"You look lost in thought." Olivia placed before Hannah a plate with one egg over easy and some whole-wheat toast with honey on the side. "And those thoughts are sad ones."

She smiled. "Who me? I'm heading off to a new adventure soon."

Olivia slid into the seat across from her. "I don't know how you do it. Picking up and going someplace new every few months. You seem to thrive on change whereas I don't."

She wished that really were the case. Hannah studied that sadness that gently etched her friend's features with pain. "Is that what you think?"

"Yes, or why would you do it? You could stay in one place. There's a need for experienced home health care providers in Billings."

To stay alive, Hannah wanted to confide to Olivia. "What's changing for you?"

Her friend bent forward, peering at the near-empty tables around them. "I'm pregnant."

"You've never mentioned a man in your life. Is there a husband? Boyfriend?"

That pain magnified Olivia's gaze even more. "I haven't spoken to my husband in months and he doesn't even…" Tears glistened in her eyes, making the powder-blue color stand out more.

"Know that you're having a baby?"

Olivia nodded.

"Is it his?"

Her friend bit her lower lip, a tear leaking out and running down her pale cheek. Again she gave a nod.

"Oh, honey, I'm so sorry. Why haven't you told him?"

"I can't contact him. I can't…" Her words came to a spattering halt. Fear chased away the pain for a few seconds. She quickly darted a look around the diner. "My husband didn't want a child."

Hannah straightened, all thoughts of her now-cool egg fleeing. "Did he abuse you? Are you running away from him?" She held her breath almost afraid of the answers.

"No, he never hurt me like that. He wouldn't. He isn't that kind of man." She peered toward the customers still in the diner. "I'm gonna move, too. I want to settle in a smaller town before the baby comes. I love children and hope I can do something with them. I'd rather do something other than be a waitress. I'd better get back to work." Olivia slid to the end of the booth and started to stand.

Hannah laid her hand over hers. "Don't leave just yet. I think you need a friend right now. Let me be that person. Where are you from?"

"Chicago."

"Does he have any idea where you are?"

Olivia shook her head.

"And you can't give him a call?"

"I won't force him into a life he doesn't want."

Hannah wanted so badly to help Olivia as best she could, to be a friend because she had so few since her plight five years ago. "It sounds like you still love him."

Her tears swimming in her eyes, Olivia bowed her head. "Yes, but it's too late for us." She lifted her gaze to Hannah's. "It's best this way. I live my life and he lives his."

"Is that what you want?"

"It doesn't matter what I want. It's irrelevant."

Hannah could identify with that. Nothing she wanted was possible for her now.

Olivia rose. "I'm moving on to a new adventure as a wise woman once said to me." A smile peeked through the sadness. "I won't forget you. Who knows? Maybe one day we'll run into each other."

"Yeah, maybe." Hannah wouldn't ask Olivia where she was going, and she wouldn't tell her friend where she was going. But before Olivia walked away, Hannah added, "You take care of yourself and your baby. I know you believe in the Lord."

"Yes."

"Then believe He'll take care of you." And Hannah prayed that were the case although in her own situation she had her doubts. She'd believed once, but now she felt abandoned, left like the Israelites when they'd wandered for years in the desert.

After Olivia returned to her waitress duties, Hannah quickly ate her cold egg and toast, got a refill on her coffee to go, then paid her check and left before she confessed why she moved around a lot. She hurried around the corner to Saul's apartment and let herself in. The older gentleman sat in the living room with his coffee on the end table next to his lounge chair.

He dropped the newspaper he was reading, shaking his head. "It's just not safe anymore. They still haven't discovered who killed those three young women. Such a shame. I wish they would assign the story to Violet Kramer. She'd get to the bottom of everything. I've been impressed with her reporting lately in my hometown paper. But I guess there's nothing this old bag of bones can do to change anything, especially since little information is being given out about the murders." Saul folded the *Missoula Daily News* into a neat pile, then stuffed it in the trash can by his side.

Hannah shrugged out of her heavy overcoat and hung it up in the hall closet before sitting on the couch across from him. She'd heard Saul grumbling every time a murder went unexplained. He was a big mystery buff and wanted to solve each case. "I've read that the police like to hold back clues to help them apprehend the killer. That's probably why we aren't getting much on the crimes." Personally she'd had her fill of anything having to do with murders.

"Yeah, I'm sure you're right." He beamed with a grin. "Your interview yesterday must have gone great. Austin called this morning when he couldn't reach you at your apartment. He figured you were here working. He wants you to call him." Saul dug in his shirt pocket and withdrew a slip of paper. "This is his cell number. He told me you could reach him anywhere with that. I hope it's good news. I tried my best to convince him and Caroline you would be perfect for the job."

"Thanks." Hannah rose, took the note and retrieved her purse on the table in the hallway to get her cell.

Staying in the foyer, her back to Saul, she punched in the numbers and waited, hoping it was good news. She needed to leave Billings soon. She'd been here too long. When Austin Taylor answered, she said, "This is Hannah Williams."

"Glad you called. I'd like you to start as soon as you can. You indicated you didn't have to give Saul a two-week notice. Is that correct?"

So formal sounding for a man who didn't stand on formalities. "No, he's fine with me leaving when I have to."

"Good. When can you get here?"

"Mr. Taylor—"

"Austin, please."

"I can come tomorrow, the same time as yesterday."

A sigh sounded. "I was hoping you would say that. Misty told me last night she wants you to live here. You made quite an impression on my daughter and grandmother."

But what was left unsaid and very clear to Hannah was that she hadn't on Austin. "I enjoyed my visit with Misty. You have a special little girl."

"Yes, I know and I almost lost her." He cleared his throat. "I'll pick you up at the bus station tomorrow then. If there is a change in plans, let me know. I carry this cell on me at all times."

"Okay. See you tomorrow." Hannah stashed her phone back into her purse and turned toward the living room.

"Today's your last day?"

Hannah nodded, hating to leave Saul. She'd become close to him. He reminded her of her grandfather, another loved one she could never see again. It was becoming harder and harder living this charade she called her life. She wanted her mother, brother, her *whole* family back. She wanted a family of her own. Perhaps for a while she could pretend while at the Triple T Ranch.

* * *

Hannah folded her last piece of clothing, put the sweater into her suitcase and closed it. Making a walk through her apartment, she couldn't find anything she'd left behind. The place already looked deserted as the other nine she'd abandoned in the past two years. This was her life now. She lived a hit-and-run existence, and there was nothing she could do about it.

The day she'd witnessed a man murder another person was the day everything changed. The shock of discovering Cullen Madison, her employer's brother and her frequent date, wasn't whom she thought he was had worn off years ago, but not the feeling that she should have known something wasn't quite right, that Cullen's business had been a front for selling arms illegally. She'd been caught up in the glamour and thrill that a handsome, rich man was interested in her. At least her testimony at his trial had put away a man the feds had wanted for a long time.

She set the soft bag on top of the bigger suitcase with rollers, pulled it to the front door and took one last look at her home for a brief time. Sadness that all she owned was with her shook her composure. Not much to account for in her thirty years but it was easy to move quickly.

Downstairs, she exited her building and scanned the area. The black SUV was parked across the street. A man sat waiting for the young woman. Impatience stamped his features. Hannah grinned and hurried her pace toward the waiting cab.

She gave the driver an address of a building near the bus depot. As the taxi turned the corner at the end of her street, she glanced back and noticed the black SUV was gone. Hopefully the woman hadn't kept him waiting too long. The thought of the two made her wonder if they were dating or just friends. She'd had few friends since she'd shed the name Jen Davis, and she certainly hadn't dated. Once when she'd still been under the U.S. Marshals' protection she'd been considering going out with a man she'd met at work. Then her life fell apart for the second time, and she'd been on the run ever since.

She tried to relax, but she couldn't—wouldn't until she had arrived at her next destination. As was her habit, she kept an eye on the traffic around the cab. Nothing out of place until the driver was a few blocks from her drop-off. That was when she spotted a black SUV just like the one in front of her apartment tucked behind a vehicle three cars back. Every nerve ending pinged to sharp awareness.

Clutching her money for the fare, she sat forward. "I changed my mind. Stop here."

When the driver complied, Hannah stuffed the twenty-dollar bill into his palm, slammed the door open, then grabbed her two pieces of luggage and bolted from the cab. Rushing toward the office building, she peered back at the black SUV at the end of the block coming toward her. Inside, she searched the foyer for an escape route. She saw a corridor that led to the suites on the ground floor. Maybe there was a back way out.

Pulling her suitcase, she hastened toward the hallway. Speed walking, she covered its length but didn't see an exit sign. With a glance over her shoulder, she turned down an offshoot of the main hall. Behind her she heard footsteps clicking on the tile floor and didn't dare look back.

Focused on the door to the staircase, she made a decision to go up if she had to. Hopefully whoever was in the black SUV wasn't really after her, or if so, they wouldn't search the whole fifteen-story building. Maybe she could find an office to hide in on another floor. Maybe she was overreacting, but she didn't want to take the chance.

In the stairwell, she zeroed in on a door on the outside wall with a red-lettered sign plastered on its dull gray surface that read Emergency Exit Only. She stared up the stairs, then at the door. If she opened it, an alarm might go off.

What choice did she really have?

None. It would be easier to get lost on the street or in another building, than in this one.

She plowed through the exit, dragging her piece of luggage while gripping her purse and small bag in her other hand. Silence greeted her as she came out into an alley between the two office buildings. Releasing her bottled breath, she glimpsed the main street where her cab had let her out and knew that wasn't the way to go. She headed deeper into the maze of alleys that ran behind and between the buildings, the odor of garbage assailing her. The smell of dead fish nearly choked her. She hastened her pace.

She kept going in the direction the bus depot was and finally emerged on the avenue that led to the station. Before taking another step, she surveyed the area for the black SUV or anything else that appeared suspicious.

Nothing.

Checking her watch, she realized she only had ten minutes to make her bus to Sweet Creek. If she thought she was in danger of being followed, she wouldn't go to the ranch. She couldn't risk their lives. She'd come up with another way to survive, to work.

With hurried steps, she approached the curb and grabbed a taxi that had just dropped off a customer. After seated in the back, she gave the driver the address of the bus depot and kept vigilance on the traffic around her. Ten minutes later, the driver stopped in front of the bus depot, and Hannah ducked inside. Again assessing the nearly deserted station, she saw nothing to alarm her.

Quickly purchasing her ticket, she strode to the bus, gave the driver her big bag, then made her way to the back by the exit, where she deposited the smaller suitcase in the seat by the window. She slid down just enough to keep an eye out the window but not be in full view of anyone on the sidewalk or in a car.

Then she watched the station and the passengers who entered the bus. She purposely forced deep air into her lungs. Her pulse rate finally slowed to a normal rate.

If there had been someone after her, then it had been a close call. Probably she overreacted, but she'd decided long ago she would rather do that than be wrong. Being wrong meant she could be dead. There was no choice.

However, the fact remained, she'd stayed too long in Billings. She'd come to care too much for Saul and allowed herself to pretend he still needed her when he hadn't. She would make sure her time at the Triple T Ranch was shorter. If there were no complications, Misty should be fine without home health care in seven or eight weeks.

Perfect for her. As much as she loved Montana and its wide-open spaces and breathtaking scenery, after this job she would have to move to another state. She really should have before now, but there was something about Montana that had touched a need in her. She wanted to stay in the state. That was a luxury, like so many others, she couldn't afford any longer.

* * *

Micah McGraw, a Deputy U.S. Marshal in Montana, picked up the phone and placed a call to his brother, Jackson, a Special Agent in the Chicago FBI field office. "I lost Hannah Williams. She must have seen me and figured I was tailing her. She bolted out of a cab and into an office building. I searched it but couldn't find her."

"Do you think Hannah Williams is Jen Davis?" Jackson asked, a tired, exasperated tone to his voice.

"Her hair's different, but that's easy enough to change. From a distance she looks like the photo I got from her file."

"Then my informant was right. I hope she left Billings then because the Martino crime family is moving in on her. There are similarities between Eloise Hill and Jen Davis that will get her killed."

"I wish the marshal who was Jen's contact hadn't retired and moved to Arizona. We could use a positive identification and someone who Jen knows. Is there any way the informant can stop them from pursuing her? Jen Davis doesn't have anything to do with the Martino crime family."

"I don't think so. The informant contacts me, not the other way around. Jen could be murdered before I speak with her again so find her, Micah. Too many have died at the hands of the Martino family."

"I'm trying. I'll keep you informed if the woman's trail is picked up." Micah replaced the receiver in its cradle and stared out the window of his office. The name of the program he was a part of mocked him. This was one witness he couldn't protect. And it certainly wasn't what he'd signed up for—watching helplessly as another was killed.

THREE

Hannah stared out the window of her bedroom at the Triple T Ranch. Big snowflakes drifted to the ground to disappear between the brown grass blades. Until she'd come to Montana she'd never seen snow and had marveled at the beauty of the landscape after it fell that first time. For a while a pristine white blanket had covered the ground and silence had reigned until a child's laugh of glee disrupted the stillness. Bundled up in layers of clothing, the boy, no more than seven, had come outside, pulling his sled toward the top of the street. In that moment she'd fallen in love with the state.

But on the long bus ride this morning, she'd firmed in her mind to leave Montana after this job. It was a big state, but she'd outlasted her welcome. Maybe she could find another place with snow that often lay undisturbed for acres and scenery that could steal her breath and make her forget everything but its beauty.

Again she would have to leave behind something she loved. Her future stretched before her in bleakness.

Turning away from the sight of the snow beginning to accumulate, Hannah opened her large suitcase and began to unpack. Dinner would be in thirty minutes and what little she had wouldn't take that long to put away. She'd finish and go get Misty. She felt so comfortable with the little girl, and maybe for a while, she could imagine Misty was her daughter.

Spending time with the child this afternoon had been the bright spot in an otherwise difficult day. Sitting in the back of the bus, she'd kept an eye on the vehicles on the highway. She was sure no one had followed her from Billings, but she would keep up her guard anyway. It was her life now whether she liked it or not.

However, the hardest time today had been driving with Austin Taylor to his ranch. When he had talked to her, it had been one question after another about her past. Questions she'd avoided as best she could. She could tell he was suspicious of her, even though a friend of the family had recommended her, which had made her wonder why he'd hired her in the first place. That had been resolved when she'd seen Caroline again. She'd hugged her as though she were a member of the family and had told her she was perfect for the job.

But not in Caroline's grandson's eyes.

She would have to remember that and especially keep her guard up around him. Every word would have to be carefully thought out.

Quickly she put her clothes in the drawer or hung them up in the closet, then she left and went into Misty's room next door. "It's snowing."

"It is? I love to play in the snow." The little girl sat in her bed, listening to her MP3 player. She removed her earplugs.

"So do I. I can't seem to get enough of it."

The corners of Misty's mouth turned down. "But I can't play in it." She slapped her hand on her leg cast.

"We'll have to talk to your dad. Maybe we can figure something out. There are a lot of ways to enjoy snow."

The expression on the little girl's face brightened. "Yeah."

"You ready for dinner?"

Misty nodded and threw back the covers. "Granny told me we're eating in the dining room tonight. We hardly ever."

"You don't?"

"No, but Granny wanted to for your first night with us."

Hannah brought the wheelchair to the side of the bed and transferred the child to it. "Show me the way."

Misty giggled. "You know it. You saw it earlier."

"Oh, I don't know. I might get lost in this big house. I'm used to a small apartment."

Her giggles increased. "Follow me." Misty guided her electric wheelchair from her room and down the hall to the foyer then the dining room. "We're here."

Austin paused in scooting his grandmother's chair in to the table that no longer sat twelve. "So you are. Here I've got a place just for you." He patted the table, halved in length, next to his seat.

While Misty maneuvered right up to her spot, Hannah sat across from the little girl with Caroline on her right. On a white tablecloth with lacy trim were ivory-colored china with gold edging, crystal goblets and gold utensils. The room mirrored Caroline's elegance.

"Daddy, can I talk?"

For a few seconds a puzzled expression crossed Austin's face before he started laughing. "This isn't Grandma Kline's. Sure you can, munchkin."

"It's snowing outside. Can I go out after dinner?"

"We'll have to protect your casts."

"That shouldn't be hard. We can throw a couple of

raincoats over both of them." Hannah unfolded her white linen napkin and spread it in her lap.

"And your father finished the ramp this afternoon." Caroline passed the platter of roast beef to Hannah.

"Great. I won't have to stay on the deck."

The smile on the little girl's face touched Hannah with joy. "The first time I saw snow I made the biggest snowman I could."

"We could make one. I love making snowmen."

"Hold on, Misty Taylor. If it's snowing, you don't need to go down that ramp. It could be slippery."

"But, Daddy, you know how I like to catch the flakes on my tongue."

"I'll carry you."

"We can make snow ice cream instead. All we need is some evaporated milk, sugar, vanilla, and a couple of eggs and, of course, snow." Hannah shifted her gaze to Caroline. "If you don't have evaporated milk, we can use regular milk. I know several ways to make it, depending on what you have on hand."

"Can we, Granny?"

Enthusiasm in Misty's voice caused Hannah to smile. "You haven't made snow ice cream before?"

The little girl shook her head. "Granny?"

"It sounds like fun. I think we have everything, even the evaporated milk."

"I don't think I ever made any. I did put a snowball in the freezer once and used it on Dad in the spring." Austin took the platter Hannah passed to him and forked several slices of the meat, then proceeded to cut some for his daughter who only had the use of one hand.

"Yes, I remember my son had a knot on his forehead after you threw it."

Misty crunched her brow in puzzlement. "Snow's soft."

"Yeah," Austin said with a chuckle, "until you put it in the freezer and it hardens into ice. I have to say Dad wasn't too happy with me, so don't try it, munchkin. I hid in the barn for the rest of the day." A faraway look entered his eyes. "I hadn't thought about that in years. The stunned look on my father's face was priceless. It was about fifty degrees, and he'd been working so hard his forehead was sweaty. I actually thought it was a good time to use the snowball."

Caroline smiled. "I never told you, but your dad thought it was, too. After you hightailed it to the barn, he burst out laughing, picked up what was left of the snowball and used it to ice his head until he could get inside and get a bag of ice."

"He did?" An incredulous expression hiked Austin's eyebrows. "He acted angry when I saw him that night."

"All a pretense." Caroline gave Hannah a bowl of potatoes, carrots and onions. "How about you? Did you ever get into a snowball fight?"

Hannah scooped the vegetables onto her plate. "No, I hadn't seen snow until I came here."

"No snow?" Misty asked with surprise.

"Not in southern California."

"So that's where you lived before coming to Montana? Where in southern California?" Austin's interrogative tone marked his words as it had in the Jeep while he drove her to the ranch earlier that day.

"Los Angeles," Hannah said, gripping her fork. She felt relatively safe with the true answer because in Los Angeles County the population was close to ten million. He'd have to dig pretty deep to come up with any information on her from that answer.

"So you grew up in L.A. before coming here. Were you a home health care provider there, too?" Austin took the rolls that Hannah handed him after snagging one for herself.

"No." She wouldn't offer any extra information unless asked, and then she would try to keep it as close to the truth as possible. She didn't want to be tripped up later with a contradictory statement. But whenever someone began asking too many questions, a headache throbbed behind her eyes.

"Austin, quit the third degree. Say grace please." Caroline bowed her head.

Both Misty and Austin followed suit. Hannah stared for a few seconds at them then dropped her gaze to her plate as Austin's deep, husky voice sounded in the stillness with a prayer of thanks for bringing Misty home safely.

Even though this was her second night at the ranch, sleep evaded Hannah as it usually did in a strange place until she felt settled in. Flipping back the covers, she rose and slipped into her terry-cloth robe, belting it as she covered the distance to the door. Yesterday Caroline had made it very clear she was to make herself at home while she was here.

And she intended to—if that were possible with Austin watching her every move. When she lived in a separate place from her patient, she had down time, which wouldn't be possible here at the ranch. She felt as though she were an actress onstage 24/7. That was why she usually had her own place.

Hannah headed for the kitchen. A hot cup of milk often helped her get to sleep. After putting a pan on the stove, she walked to the window to watch the snow continue to fall. She loved seeing that, and since she would soon be gone from Montana, she would enjoy it as much as she could.

"Can't sleep?"

Austin's deep, husky voice startled her, spinning her around so fast she nearly lost her balance. She clutched the counter nearby and steadied herself. "I didn't hear you come in."

"Sorry. I took my boots off." He pointed to his feet clad in socks. "I was going upstairs to bed when I saw the light on in the kitchen. I thought the cook had left it on."

"Rene is a very good cook. The meal tonight was as delicious as last night's."

His gaze shifted to the stove, a question in his eyes.

"Couldn't sleep so I'm heating some milk."

"That works?"

"Yes—at least for me it does. I don't like taking any pills to help me sleep." They would make her too groggy if she had to get up fast and think of an escape plan. She still remembered the other night when she had awakened from the nightmare, and it had taken her a few moments to get her bearing. And that had been without any aids to help her sleep.

"I'll have to give it a try. I usually just work in the office until I can't keep my eyes open. Tonight even that isn't working."

"What's on your mind?" Hannah walked to the refrigerator and grabbed the milk to pour some more into the pan.

He shrugged. "Stuff. I don't want to bore you with the running of the ranch."

After she added more milk, she put the carton back in the fridge. "I can't imagine running a ranch being boring."

He smiled, the gesture encompassing his whole face. "It isn't really. Not to me."

"But something must be bothering you." *Is it me?*

"I found a cigarette butt in the barn today, which means that one of my hired hands is smoking on the job. I've always insisted if you're going to work at the Triple T that you don't smoke on the job and especially in the barn. It's a fire hazard with all the hay around." He leaned against the counter near the sink, kneading his nape. "I've never had a problem with it until now."

"Have you hired anyone new?"

"A couple. Rodney has been here since January and Cal I took on a few weeks ago. I got the impression from both men they didn't smoke."

"They might not have wanted to say anything to you in order to get the job. I'd take a look at them first. Does anyone you know who works for you smoke?"

"Three. But it's never been a problem. In fact, I think Kevin quit this past year."

When the milk was heated, Hannah poured two mugs full of the hot liquid then gave one to Austin. "Any visitors lately?"

"Besides you? No. Not for a week."

"Thankfully you can rule me out since I just arrived. I don't smoke and I haven't left the house except when we all went out front for Misty yesterday evening. All you can do is keep an eye on the new guys and check out the ones you know smoke. Of course, it's possible someone just started or never told you."

Austin folded his long length into the chair at the oak table in the kitchen. "I've already questioned all my employees. Everyone denies it is his cigarette."

"Then one of them is lying to you."

"Yeah, I can put up with a lot, but lying isn't one of them. I've found the truth always comes out in the end."

Hannah dropped her gaze to her milk. She hoped her "truth" didn't come out in the end. She didn't know how to stay safe and not lie about who she was.

"Now when I discover who it is, I'll have to fire him."

"No second chance?"

"I could have excused the smoking in the barn but not the lying about it. I could never trust that person again and trust is important to me." Austin's intense gaze drilled into Hannah.

She resisted the urge to squirm in her seat. Quickly she lifted the mug to her lips to give herself something to do. But over its rim, her eyes locked with his, and she couldn't look away as though he'd roped her to him.

Putting her drink on the table, she finally dragged her gaze away. "Well, I hope you catch the culprit. I can image the damage a lit cigarette can do in a barn with all that hay and wood."

"And miles from the nearest help. We do have some fire hoses we can use and a water source, mostly to keep one from spreading. If a barn is set on fire, it can be difficult to stop. When I was a child and my father was still alive, our barn caught on fire, and it burned to the ground in two hours. There was nothing my dad could do to save it. Some of the animals even died in it. I never want to go through that again."

"I haven't had a pet in years, but when I did and something happened to her, I grieved as though a member of the family had died."

"That's the way Misty feels about Candy and our dog, Barney, that stays at the barn." He grinned, two dimples appearing. "Actually I'm kinda partial to Barney myself. He's been around for twelve years."

"Didn't I see a kennel off the barn?"

"Yeah, I have dogs that work the cattle. Barney used to when he was younger. Now arthritis has set in, and he doesn't move as fast, but he sure can bark. Best watch-dog." Austin took a sip of his milk. "So what kind of pet did you have?"

"Cats. I've always had them."

"But not now."

It wasn't a question because if she had a cat now it would be with her, but for some reason she felt she needed to make a comment. "As you know, I travel around a lot. It becomes difficult taking an animal with me and occasionally I've lived at a place like I am here, so it wouldn't be a good idea to have a pet."

"Do you miss having one?"

"Yes." That was an answer from the heart. Every day she missed Callie, her last cat she'd left behind when she'd fled the Witness Protection setup. Risking being caught, she'd stopped at a house of a coworker who loved cats and left Callie with her. She would be thirteen now. Callie used to listen to her problems and just holding her and petting her would make things better. Hannah had nothing to help her now, and there were times she felt as if she were going to fall apart from the stress and heartache.

"We have a cat that stays in the barn. She's been with us for a year. Great mouser. She and Barney get along great. You should go down there and meet Snowball. Misty named her. Snowball appeared one day in the barn during winter in the middle of a snowstorm."

"Can I take Misty to the barn? That is, if this snow doesn't last long."

"Sure. One of my ranch hands clears the snow fairly fast around the house and barn. A visit to the barn might brighten her mood. My daughter is an active little girl, and lately her activities have been curtailed drastically."

Hannah finished her milk. "I'll see what I can do about that."

"According to my grandmother, you're just the person to accomplish that." Rising, Austin grabbed her empty mug and his and took them to the sink. "The first decent day, I'll have to show you around the ranch."

"On a horse?"

He faced her, eyeing her. "Is that panic in your voice?"

"I've never been on a horse, so I doubt that would be the best way to see the ranch." The thought of getting on a horse didn't appeal to her at all.

"Actually I have several motorized vehicles I use here at the ranch."

"Then Misty could go?"

"Yeah, although her favorite way to see the ranch is on Candy." He lounged back against the counter, clasping the edge of it on either side of him.

"Seeing her with Candy yesterday evening, I certainly understand. Her whole face transformed when you brought the mare up for your daughter to pet."

"I hope nothing happens to Candy. Misty couldn't take another death."

"I can imagine." Her mother was alive but knowing she would never be able to see her bereaved her as if her mom had passed away. "I'm so sorry to hear about your wife dying. Misty said it makes you sad when she talks about her."

Austin flinched. "Not sad. More like angry. Not at my daughter but Jillian. If she hadn't taken her that night, Misty wouldn't be in the situation she's in right now." He shook his head as though ridding himself of some unwanted image and pushed off from the counter. "I think your milk remedy is working. I need to head to bed. Tomorrow will be here soon enough."

With a glance at the clock over the stove, Hannah rose. Although Austin tried to suppress his anger toward his wife by wiping any from his expression, it flowed off him in waves, the tension in his body palpable.

"And my daughter wakes up early."

"I gathered that from this morning. I'm an early riser, too."

"Even when you go to bed at three?"

"Yes, even then. It takes me a while to get used to a new place. This is normal for me."

At the end of the hallway near her bedroom, he angled toward her. "Then why don't you stay in one place?"

If only I could. I would gladly give up this lifestyle to put roots down in one place. "I fill a need." Which really wasn't an answer. She could see in his eyes he wasn't satisfied by the reply. She forced a yawn. "I think the milk's working for me, too. Good night," she quickly said and hurried toward her room before he pursued the reason for her wanderlust.

She closed the door and leaned back against it, breathing deep inhalation to calm the galloping of her heartbeat. It was too easy to talk to Austin when he wasn't in his interrogation mode. For a while in the kitchen she'd forgotten her past and was totally into the moment with him.

I can't do it. I've got to keep my guard up.

For a second she thought of praying to the Lord for strength to keep going with her charades. But then, why should she? He hadn't answer her last prayers in Los Angeles or when she'd first come to Montana. Obviously she wasn't worthy of His attention.

* * *

As the first rays of light spread across the landscape the next morning, in the barn Misty presented her flat palm with a piece of an apple in it to Candy. When the horse plucked the treat from her hand, the little girl giggled. “She always tickles me with her nose.”

Hannah inched closer to the stall door. In an area no bigger than ten by ten feet being confined with a horse, even a small one, wasn’t her idea of something fun to do. But it was Misty’s and that was why Hannah would stay. Her heart tapped a mad staccato, however, against her chest.

“This was the bestest idea, Hannah.”

“We’ll probably need to be getting back before your dad and Caroline wonder where we went before breakfast.”

“Can we come back later today? I like coming to the barn better than Daddy bringing Candy up to the house.”

“Yeah, that is if it doesn’t snow. The sky was pretty gray. And of course, if it’s okay with your father.”

“It’s not gonna snow, and Daddy will be fine about it.” Misty’s expression mirrored all her hope that sounded in her voice. “Before the wreck, I always got to feed Barney. Can we before we go?”

“Sure. Where’s the food?”

“In the storage room.” Misty nestled her face against Candy’s head.

“Will you be okay while I go get it?”

Misty laughed. “Nuthin’ gonna happen with Candy here.”

Although Hannah had tried to keep her fear of large animals she was unfamiliar with from her voice, the amused look the little girl gave her along with what she said underscored her failure. At the stall entrance Hannah glanced back over her shoulder at Misty and Candy. The mare kept her head lowered so the child could continue to pet her as if the horse knew something was wrong with Misty, that the child couldn't stand. No, Misty would be fine, and Hannah would have to get used to Candy because weather willing she planned on bringing the girl down to the barn a lot. Misty came alive in here.

When she checked her watch, Hannah realized they had stayed longer than she had planned. She could picture Austin combing the house for them, anger building on his face when he didn't find them. Hurrying toward what she believed was the storage room, she burst through the closed door and came to an abrupt halt.

A small, wiry man with his back to her stood in the corner by some boxes. As he swung his gaze to her, surprise flittered into his expression. He made a scraping movement with his foot then whirled around. "What are you doing in here?"

His furious tone caused her to step back into the doorway of the storage room, the faint odor of smoke accosting her. "I'm getting Barney's food," she said and spied the bag several feet from the man. "Misty's going to feed him."

Some of the tension in him deflated. "Oh, I just didn't expect anyone to come in here at this hour. I'll bring it out to you."

His dismissal of her heightened her suspicion. He was probably the hired hand who was smoking in the barn. She couldn't ignore the faint odor of cigarette smoke. This wasn't any of her business. She needed to back out of the room and dismiss what he had been doing. Getting involved and doing the right thing five years ago ruined her life. Austin would discover the guy soon enough.

What if Austin didn't and something happened? For the past years, she had done what she needed to survive, but she couldn't turn a blind eye to what this man was doing. If the man flicked the cigarette into some hay, the barn could be destroyed. Animals killed.

"That's all right. I can get it." She headed toward the bag on the floor, forcing the hired hand to move.

His glare chilled her. He stepped to the side, planting one foot and dragging the other to him. The scent of smoke hanging in the air was stronger the closer she came to him, confirming her suspicions.

Hannah bent over to lift the twenty-five-pound bag but almost instantly dropped it back to the floor. "On second thought, could you please carry this bag out to Misty? It's heavier than I thought." Straightening, she watched his every action.

Austin's employee pawed the wooden planks with the toe of his boot, then reluctantly covered the space between them and scooped up the bag as though it only weighed a few pounds. "After you, ma'am."

Near the entrance Hannah stopped. "Oh, I forgot the cat food. You go ahead. I can manage that bag." She sidled away, backing up toward where she saw the cat food.

The man grumbled something under his breath, but he left. Hannah rushed to where he had been standing and searched the floor. Nothing. He had to be smoking. Unless he came in right after someone had just finished. Doubt began to nibble at her when she zeroed in on the tip of the cigarette butt under the shelving where he'd shoved it with his booted foot.

She pulled it out and murmured, "Gotcha."

Someone cleared his throat behind her.

FOUR

The sudden unexpected sound behind her caused Hannah to whirl, the cigarette butt clutched between her thumb and forefinger. The doorway framed Austin's tall, muscular build. A frown carved his features in stone. His flintlike gaze locked on the cigarette and his eyes flared.

"This isn't mine," she quickly said.

"Where did you find that?" The frost in his look carried over into his voice.

Hannah pointed to the floor by the shelving. "Under there."

"Why did you look under there?"

"Because when I came in here, a cowhand was acting suspiciously and I could smell smoke."

Austin approached. "Who?"

"I don't know who. He was thin but strong-looking. Had brown hair, gray eyes. Short, maybe five-six. He took a bag of dog food so Misty and I could feed Barney." She started forward. "I need to get back to Misty. She's with Candy."

As she passed Austin, a hand on her arm stopped her. "I'd like the butt." He laid his palm out flat for her. "And Misty is right outside the door."

"You didn't see anyone with Barney's food?"

"No, but I imagine he hightailed it out of here."

"So, you know who it is?" She put the cigarette into his hand and watched as he curled his fingers around it, so tightly that the tips reddened.

"One of the guys I took on in the fall. I'll be tracking him down later."

Hannah didn't doubt that. His anger vibrated the air between them. The hired hand had lied to Austin, and he didn't take kindly to that fact. Thankfully she only had to be here seven or eight weeks because she never wanted him to know her whole life was a lie. She suppressed a shudder.

He released his hold, and Hannah took a step toward the door, then came to a halt. "I almost forgot. I need the cat food, too."

"You go ahead. I'll get it."

Quickly she left him. The storage room was way too small for the both of them. Although it was cold in the barn, sweat dampened her undershirt. She found Misty near the metal bowls for Barney and Snowball. The white cat rubbed himself against Misty's uninjured leg while the little girl patted Barney, a mixture of probably four or five large breeds with long brown hair and a tail that wagged enthusiastically.

"I see your pets are ready to eat." Hannah spied the bag of dog food propped up against the wall by the dishes.

"I'm a little early to feed them today. They sure miss me." Snowball leaped into Misty's lap, her giggles mingling with her pet's loud purring.

"Yes, I can see that. My cat would rub herself against my face and like to drape herself around my neck. Of course, it was hard to breathe sometimes so I had to put a stop to that."

Misty tilted her head to the side. “What happened to your cat?”

“I left her with a friend.”

“You shouldn’t be away from her. We have plenty of room for a cat, don’t we, Daddy?” The girl’s gaze fixed on her father behind Hannah.

When she rotated toward Austin, she wished she hadn’t said anything about Callie. Misty had a way of making her forget she had to watch her every word and guard what she revealed.

He dropped the bag of food next to the other one and straightened. “Sure, if you want.”

“I won’t be here long. I hate to move Callie around too much, and she loves the children at my friend’s house.” Which was all true thankfully.

“I’ll share Snowball with you.”

Misty’s words swelled Hannah’s throat with emotions she wanted to deny. In just a few days she was growing to care too much for this little girl she would have to leave. Hannah swallowed several times and said, “That’s so sweet of you.”

“Here, hold her.” Misty tried to pick Snowball up with her one good arm and because the cat weighed about fifteen pounds she couldn’t manage.

Hannah rushed to the child and took Snowball. “Thanks.” She pressed the animal against her chest and scratched him behind his ears. The sound of his purrs brought back memories of Callie and nights that she spent talking to her pet about her mother and brother. Callie had been a willing listener to her woes and had met a need in Hannah to talk about her pain at leaving them behind. She’d cried many tears to Callie. Burying her face in Snowball’s fur, she kept her head down while she fought the tears so close to the surface as the memories tumbled through her.

At the sound of the dry bits falling into the metal bowl, Barney bolted to his dish and began to eat. Reluctantly Hannah placed Snowball on the ground as Austin filled his bowl. Misty moved closer and watched both animals eating while Austin took the bags back into the storage room.

When he came out, he shut the door then locked it. "I came down here to get you two. Breakfast is probably ready by now."

"Good. I'm starved." Misty turned her electric wheelchair and headed for the main house.

Hannah followed with Austin next to her. "Did you find any other cigarette butts in the storage room?"

"Yeah, a stash. How did you know I had?"

"You locked the door. It hadn't been locked previously."

"I don't go in there much. Most of what I need is in the tack room over there." He gestured toward another door near the entrance as they left the barn. "I'll give you a key so you can get the food for the pets."

She spared a glance toward him, his strong jawline set in a clench. "What are you going to do about the cowhand?"

"Fire him. First, he has no business being in the barn at that hour. He's been neglecting his duties. I was hoping over time he would settle into the job, but he hasn't. I need someone who will work. And lastly, he lied to me, point-blank. Those are all reasons I'm letting him go. If it had just been the smoking, we could have worked something out. I can't trust him."

"And that's important to you," she murmured, almost

as though she needed to remind herself that he was off limits for many reasons but that was one of them.

"Isn't it to you?" He slowed his pace.

"Yeah, trust is important in a relationship." She couldn't cover the wistful tone in her voice.

He came to a stop and faced her. "It sounds like you've been burned before."

"Yes." She had no intention of telling him how she'd been burned, so she kept moving toward the house and hoped for a reprieve from all his inquiries even though they weren't always phrased as questions. When he caught up with her, she decided to do her own probing. "How about you? Have you been burned?" She wondered about Misty's mother and the few remarks the child had made about her.

His stony look and the tension emanating from him made it obvious he wasn't going to answer.

"I'm sorry. I shouldn't have asked. But Misty has said a few things. I thought if I knew what happened the night of the car wreck I could help her better. But I can understand the pain and grief you're going through. It wouldn't be easy talking about your deceased wife." And she needed to remind herself his wife had died five weeks before. That ought to take care of any attraction she felt toward Austin.

He rolled his shoulders. "What has she been saying?"

"She misses her mommy and is worried about you. Sometimes I get the impression she thinks she caused the wreck. Not from anything she's said exactly, but something's bothering her."

He peered toward his daughter, who was maneuvering her wheelchair up the ramp to the deck in front. As he watched his grandmother let Misty into the house, myriad emotions flitted in and out of his eyes—puzzlement, sadness and finally a resolve. "My wife and I had been separated a year when she returned to the ranch to take Misty away. We fought about it. That was the first time she had come back since she'd left. She'd talked to our daughter a few times on the phone but that was all. I thought I'd made myself clear. She wanted to read a bedtime story to Misty. Then she said she would leave. I received an important call I'd been waiting for. I went into my office, leaving the door open to listen for Jillian coming out of Misty's room and down the stairs. When you step on a certain stair, it creaks. I didn't count on Jillian sneaking Misty out of the house because she hadn't really shown any interest in our daughter." The monotone he used to tell his story, his faraway stare underscored how difficult it was to talk about what happened that night.

Hannah wanted to end the pain it produced. "You don't have—"

"The next thing," Austin continued in a tightly controlled voice, "I know is Granny telling me Misty was gone. I jumped into the Jeep to go after them." He removed his cowboy hat and plowed his fingers through his hair, a tic in his cheek twitching. "I found the wreck ten minutes later."

Without thinking, Hannah touched his arm. "I'm so sorry."

He plopped his hat on his head and shrugged his arm away. "It shouldn't have happened." He started to say something else but instead clamped his mouth shut and stalked up the steps to the deck.

Hannah blew a breath out. Who was he angry with, himself or his wife?

At the door he halted, his hand on the knob. "I would

rather you not talk about the wreck with Misty unless she brings it up, then answer what questions you need but don't dwell on it. She doesn't remember a lot about it or the first few days right after it. I don't want her reliving it." Because he did enough for the both of them. He dreamed about the wreck, often waking up in a sweat with images of his daughter crumpled like a broken doll.

He wrenched open the door and entered his house, very aware of the woman coming inside right behind him. She'd kept him up late, too. There was something about her—a vulnerability—that nibbled at his defenses. When Jillian had left him over a year ago, he'd promised himself he wouldn't give his heart to another. Living on the ranch wasn't for everyone, and he didn't have the time to go out looking for a woman who would love the ranch, his daughter and him as well as the Lord. That was a tall order and one he didn't intend to try to fill.

Then Hannah arrived to help with Misty. They instantly connected better than his daughter had with her own mother. He'd heard more laughter and talking from Misty in the past few days since Hannah had come than he had in months when Jillian had lived here.

"Austin?"

Hannah's voice with a huskiness to it melted the ice about his emotion. He slowed his pace across the large foyer and peered back at her, standing in the threshold to the dining room. "Yes."

"Aren't you going to eat breakfast?"

He gave a quick shake of his head and continued his trek to his office. He was afraid if he was around Hannah anymore he would spill his guts to her. And he had a man to fire.

* * *

Austin stuck his head in the doorway to Misty's room later that day. "You've got a call."

Hannah clenched the book she was reading to the child. "A call?" *Who knows I'm here?* Fear mushroomed through her. Beads of perspiration coated her forehead.

"Yeah, Saul called and talked to my grandmother, then wanted to talk to you." He covered the distance to the bed. "I'll finish up in here. Granny is in the kitchen."

Hannah breathed a sigh of relief, leaned over and kissed Misty's cheek. "Good night. Don't let the bed bugs bite."

The little girl giggled. "I won't."

Hannah hurried from the child's bedroom. When she entered the kitchen, Caroline waved her over to the desk where she sat talking on the phone.

"Saul, Hannah is here. It was nice catching up with you. You need to call more often, or maybe when you feel like it, come see us at the ranch." She paused a half a minute. "Yeah, I will. Bye." Caroline handed the receiver to her, then pushed herself to her feet and moved toward the door.

"Hi, Saul. Is everything okay?" Hannah wiped one palm on her jeans, then switched the phone to the other hand and did the same thing.

"Can't a friend call and make sure you got to the ranch all right?"

"Well, yeah." It had been so long since she'd had someone care about her like that. The gesture touched her heart. "I'm fine. Misty and I are hitting it off. She's adorable."

"Caroline was telling me about what a great job you're doing." Saul cleared his throat. "I also wanted to tell you something I found out today when I went to Mama's Diner for lunch. It had been a while since I'd been there with my illness and all. But the lady who owns Mama's Diner is a friend."

"You told me about Alice when I first came to work for you. That's why I started going there for breakfast."

"Alice told me something interesting. She'd been gone a while because her granddaughter had a baby and she went to Missoula to see her."

Hannah sank onto the chair at the desk. Saul loved to tell his stories and sometimes they took a while. "That's great."

"Anyway, that's not what I called about. She had a woman and a man come in a couple of weeks ago. It turns out it was Violet Kramer. You know, the reporter I told you about that I like to follow in my hometown newspaper."

"It's a small world. Too bad you couldn't meet her."

"Alice said Violet asked her about a woman named Jen Davis. She wondered if this Jen ever came into the diner, if she lived or worked around the area. Alice said she didn't know anyone by that name, but when Violet showed her a photo, Alice thought it looked like you some."

Hannah straightened. Her grip on the receiver tightened. "Looked like me?"

"Yeah, but the quality wasn't great so Alice wasn't sure."

"Did she say anything about me to the reporter?" Hannah asked in as nonchalant voice as she could muster while her heartbeat accelerated when she thought of the ramifications if a reporter found out who she was and where she lived.

Saul chuckled. "Alice didn't say a word. She isn't partial to nosey reporters, and besides, she wasn't sure herself. I assured her your name wasn't Jen Davis, but I thought you'd get a kick out of the fact you've got a look-alike out there who Violet is looking for. She isn't your usual nosey reporter. When I've read her recent articles, she cares about the people she writes about. If there's a reporter you could trust, it would be her."

"That is funny." Hannah forced a lightness into her voice. "I'm sure somewhere there's someone who looks exactly like you."

"Oh, that poor man." His laughter drifted through the connection. "Anyway, I mainly wanted to make sure you arrived all right and the job was working out."

"Thanks, Saul. You're a good friend." After Hannah hung up, she remained at the desk, staring at the phone. A reporter was looking for her. Why? Did it have something to do with what happened in LA.?

On Saturday night Hannah tucked Misty into bed and settled beside the young girl to read her a story. "Which one would you like to hear?"

"The one about the princess." The child tried to stifle a yawn but couldn't. She laid her head against Hannah's shoulder.

She began and got through one page when Misty's head fell forward. Hannah eased up from the bed and covered the girl to her chin. After Hannah tiptoed to the bookcase and shelved the book, she came back to switch off the lamp, leaving only the nightlight for illumination. The instant the lamp went out, Misty's eyes popped open.

"You leaving?" She yawned again, blinking rapidly as she fought to stay awake.

"Well, no, I don't have to. I can sit here until you fall asleep if you want."

"Yes," Misty whispered and snuggled deeper into the covers. "Will you promise me somethin'?"

"Yes, if I can." Hannah sat again on the bed beside Misty.

"I get to go to church tomorrow. Will you come?"

She'd used to go to church with her mother every week. Often her younger brother would accompany them. But that changed when she'd witnessed the murder. She hadn't attended church since the whole mess that landed her in the Witness Protection Program began. And she wasn't sure she should. Five years ago she gave up asking the Lord for anything. She suspected now He wasn't too happy with her. But how was she supposed to believe in a loving God if He didn't care about what happened to her and for that matter her mother and brother with her disappearance?

"Hannah, will you?"

She looked toward the little girl whose milk-chocolate eyes were glued to her, worry in their depths. Hannah brushed a lock of hair from her face. "Yes, I'll come with you. So you're pretty excited about going to church?"

"I haven't seen my friends in *ages.*"

Hannah's fond memories of belonging to a congregation and seeing people she cared about each week engulfed her in sadness of all she'd lost. "It'll be fun meeting them." She forced a light tone into her voice.

A huge smile faded quickly as Misty yawned yet again. Her eyelids slid close. "You'll like them. Jamie's my best..."

The last part of the child's sentence faded into the silence as sleep finally swept through her. Hannah stared at Misty, her throat tight. If she had a little girl, she wish—*Stop it!* She couldn't do the what-ifs. She wasn't going to have a child. Although the ache in her heart burned in her chest, she could never risk it. Ever. The walls of her own prison closed in on her.

"Hannah, are you all right?"

Austin's voice from the doorway jerked her from her thoughts. She glanced down at her hands interlocked so tightly her knuckles whitened. She unlaced her fingers and swung her attention toward Misty's father.

He took a step toward her. "Is Misty okay?"

She dredged up a smile of reassurance. "Yes, she's fine. She just asked me to go to church with her tomorrow." Not wanting to wake the child, she pushed to her feet and quickly covered the distance between her and Austin. "I told her I would. That's all right, isn't it?"

"Of course, you can go with us." He touched her elbow and guided her into the hall. "But do you really want to go?"

"I don't know. I…" The pressure in her chest, as if those prison walls had closed totally in on her and were squeezing the last breath from her lungs, made it difficult to talk. She backed away, then spun on her heel and hurried toward her room next to Misty's.

Shutting her door, she listened for his footsteps to recede down the hallway, but quiet mocked her need to grieve her loss of family and freedom for the past five years. She wanted to hold a loved one. She wanted a family. The last child she had taken care of hadn't been a live-in situation. She hadn't been a part of the family. She'd put in her shift with the boy and left. Here she couldn't do that. She didn't even have a means of transportation to leave the ranch for a break.

Tears smarted her eyes. This job hadn't been a good move for her. She'd thought the isolation would be a plus.

She wouldn't have to watch every car or person coming into her view. But she'd only traded one set of problems for another—far worse because they played with her emotions, her deep need to have more than the life dealt her.

Hannah leaned back against her door and closed her eyes, keeping the sobs inside. She tried to imagine her mother and younger brother. Suddenly their images wouldn't appear on the screen of her mind. Instead she pictured Austin, tall, commanding, holding his daughter's hand and reaching out toward Hannah.

She sank to the floor and buried her face in her hands. The tears came then, flowing unchecked.

Austin stared at the closed door to Hannah's bedroom. His hands curled and uncurled at his sides. He wanted to burst into her room and hold her. He'd seen raw pain in her eyes.

Why these feelings? What's going on, Lord? I don't want to care about anyone.

The sound of crying filtered through the wooden barrier between them. He stepped forward. Halted. She was hurting. What had happened to make her cry? Why would Misty asking her to go to church cause this? He gritted his teeth, wanting so badly to pound on her door until she let him in.

He hated secrets. They had destroyed his marriage. He felt Hannah's whole life was a secret. And yet, she drew him. He'd catch a certain look of pain in her eyes that spoke to his own. He saw how she interacted with his daughter and saw genuine caring on her part—more than Misty's own mother had ever given her.

What do I do, Lord? I'm not very good at relationships. I couldn't even keep my wife here at the ranch.

Finally silence surrounded him as though that were his answer. This wasn't the right time. Hannah needed her privacy, but he intended to discover what was going on with her. And maybe he'd be able to show her there was a higher power who could help her better than anyone.

He moved toward his daughter's room, tiptoeing across it to her bed. Bending down, he kissed her softly. Misty was his life now.

After the service at Sweet Creek Christian Church, Hannah walked beside Misty while her dad pushed her toward the recreation hall in a manual wheelchair that was easy to transport. The reverend had made a point to ask Caroline and Austin to stay for refreshments.

She'd gone with Misty to her Sunday school class before the service and met all the girl's friends. She'd even enjoyed the older couple who taught the children a lesson on the Ten Commandments. But when she'd sat between Austin and Misty, positioned at the end of the pew, she felt like a fraud, listening to the reverend's sermon on trust in the Lord. She'd lost the ability to trust anyone or anything.

She couldn't forget the man's parting words from the Psalms: *God is our refuge and strength, a very present help in trouble.* If only that were the case.

Caroline opened one of the double doors into the rec hall while another person thrust the other wide. Austin wheeled Misty through the threshold. The sound of cheering and clapping greeted the child's entrance. A twelve-foot-long banner on the far wall proclaimed "Welcome back, Misty," and a large sheet cake and a bowl of red punch graced a long table.

The little girl beamed at the scene before her. The sight

of the child's happiness expanded Hannah's chest. She almost felt as if she was being welcomed into the midst of these people.

"This is for me," Misty murmured, her gaze sweeping the room filled with parishioners.

"Yup, munchkin." Austin leaned down. "You're special to these people."

Hannah backed away as the children from Misty's class surrounded her, so pleased with themselves for keeping a secret about the party. Hannah stood by the double doors, nodding to a few parishioners who greeted her but perfectly content to be away from the crowd.

"This is what Misty needed," Caroline said as she approached Hannah. "I had no idea they were going to surprise her like this."

"Yeah, the joy on her face is wonderful to watch." Pure, innocent joy, something Hannah wished she could remember. When was the last time she'd laughed without a care in the world?

"It's good to see Austin smiling more, too."

"I imagine this whole thing has been hard on him."

"If it hadn't been for the Lord, I don't know if he would have made it. He came apart at the hospital. The sheriff told him that if Misty had been sitting just a half a foot to the left she would probably have died like Jillian. When his daughter came out of the operation, I found him in the chapel on his knees, tears streaking down his cheeks."

Such love. "I'm glad God answered his prayers."

Caroline studied her a moment. "It sounds like you think He didn't answer yours."

Hannah shook her head.

Caroline turned toward her and took her hands. "He answered mine. I wanted someone special to work with

Misty and we have someone like that. The Lord always answers your prayers in His time, but His reply might not be what you think it should be."

Hannah attempted a smile that she couldn't maintain. "What if you don't like His answer?"

"Have you asked yourself why?"

Oh, many times. Why am I away from my family? Why am I hiding and scared all the time?

"Keep praying. Don't give up. He hears you." Caroline squeezed Hannah's hands. "All I know is that I'm so glad you are with us. Now I'm going to relieve my grandson for a while. I need to get in on the celebration." She started toward the crowd around Misty, stopped and peered back. "Coming?"

"I will in a minute."

But as Hannah watched the group, she felt like she always did since coming to Montana—an outsider yearning to be accepted. She rotated toward the door and pulled it open. Out in the foyer she inhaled then exhaled deep breaths, but still felt as if a band was constricting her chest. Too many emotions churned through her, threatening her composure.

Her gaze swept the area as she tried to decide where to go. Her attention fell upon the glass doors into the sanctuary. The empty place called to her, and she moved toward it. Inside the church, she slipped into the back pew and sat.

Lord, why have You abandoned me? I tried to do the right thing, and I'm the one who's being punished. I didn't kill that man. Why me? What do You want from me? Did I not believe hard enough?

Question after question reeled through her mind, but answers evaded her. Adrift on a sea of doubt, she floundered, trying to grasp hold of something to keep her afloat.

A sensation of being watched sent her heart pounding. She scanned the church then looked to the side and behind her. Out in the foyer stood Austin, his gaze on her. He nodded but stayed where he was as though he was there to protect her privacy. Another brick in her wall about her emotions crumbled into dust.

When Hannah entered the kitchen later Sunday evening after everyone else was asleep, the phone on the desk snagged her attention. Her curiosity aroused, she couldn't get Saul's call the other day out of her mind. Why was Violet looking for Jen Davis? She hadn't used that name in years. She could call her on her cell and block her number. It would be hard to track her, especially since she didn't leave her cell on. She only turned it on when she needed to make a call.

Hannah opened the refrigerator. Cold air enveloped her, along with the thought she should douse her curiosity. She should leave it alone. But what if the woman kept asking questions and searching for her? That could bring attention to her and get her killed.

"I thought I'd find you in here." Austin entered the kitchen later Sunday evening after everyone else was asleep and planted himself not far from Hannah, leaning back against the counter. "I always check on Misty before going to bed and saw your door was open and your room empty."

She sent him a smile, pushing the thought of Violet Kramer from her mind. "I checked on her before coming in here." Lifting the milk carton, she asked, "Do you want any?"

"Sure. I never thought I would acquire a taste for warm milk, but it did the trick the other night."

After filling the pan, Hannah stirred the liquid, glad to have something to do with her hands. She couldn't get Austin's look in the church's foyer out of her mind. Protective as though with him she was safe. That feeling had stayed with her all day. When she had finally left the sanctuary, Austin had disappeared into the rec hall, not saying a word to her as though he'd instinctively realized she'd needed some space to process her conflicting emotions concerning the Lord.

When the silence between them lengthened to a full minute, she shifted and faced him partially. "You never told me if you talked with the man who had been smoking in the barn."

"Not yet. I kept missing him on Friday. He was off this weekend, and I want to do this in person. This incident with the smoking only confirmed what I needed to do a couple of weeks ago. He doesn't do his job well, and I need everyone pulling his weight. I'll tell him tomorrow."

"So he isn't one of the hands who lives on the ranch?"

"No, I'll have to fill his vacancy soon."

After Hannah poured some milk into two mugs that Austin retrieved from the cabinet, she sat at the table with him across from her. "Misty couldn't stop talking about the surprise party for her this afternoon."

"It tired her out, though."

"Yeah, her stamina isn't back to its usual level, but she took an extra long nap today."

"How's Granny doing?" He sipped his drink.

"I'm watching her sugar levels and what she eats. I hope to get her to go for walks with me while Misty is napping. Exercise helps."

"My grandmother used to ride a lot. Maybe I should suggest she start again. You two could do that."

"Remember I don't ride."

"I could give you a few lessons so you could keep up with Granny."

She laughed, a picture of her up on a large horse flashing into her mind. "I think I'll stick to walking or using one of your motorized vehicles. I can see some of the ranch that way."

"But you're limited where you can go. Some of the views that overlook the ranch are gorgeous."

"I'll think about it." *For about two seconds,* she added silently.

"Chicken."

"Are you challenging me?" Lifting the mug, she took a drink.

"Is it working?"

"Why do you want to teach me?"

He kneaded the back of his neck, his head tilted. "You know, I don't know. I love to ride, especially on the ranch, and I guess I just wanted to share that with you. You're always with Misty and when you aren't you're making sure Granny is all right. You're putting in more than an eight-hour day."

"I enjoy helping both of them. Your family is special." The last word caught in her throat when she thought of all three of them and how in a short time she had come to care a lot for them. Even before she had arrived at the ranch she'd heard stories from Saul about the Taylors, especially about Austin when he was young. That last day with Saul had been filled with information concerning them, producing a yearning in her she hadn't realized until she'd settled in and observed the loving connection between them. She swallowed several gulps of her milk, feeling its warmth slide down her throat.

"Yeah, I'm fortunate to have both my grandmother and daughter in my life. When Misty was in the hospital, I realized how close I'd come to losing her, and it was—hard on me."

"But with therapy, she'll be good as new, running, playing as if the wreck hadn't happened." And she would miss seeing Misty doing that. That bothered her enough that she even contemplated staying in Montana for a few extra months and visiting Misty come summer to see how she was progressing. She couldn't do that, but she wanted to.

"The doctor said she might have problems for a long time with her breathing. But it could have been so much worse."

"How did you deal with it? I can't even imagine putting myself into your shoes."

"With a lot of praying. That's all I could do. The rest was in the Lord's hands."

"What if someone does do that and nothing happens?"

"Then perhaps you got an answer. It may not be what you were looking for, though."

To live the life I am? No, I wouldn't wish that on anyone. But then the alternative would have been a murderer going free. How could I have lived with that? There was no easy answer.

She finished the last few sips of her drink, then rose and took her mug to the sink. "I'd better call it a night and hope this works."

She turned from the counter and almost collided into Austin behind her. A gasp escaped her lips. She hadn't heard him move. The thought that he could come up on her like that highlighted her vulnerability. Her pulse sped as he reached around her and placed his cup on the counter. His fresh, clean fragrance, like the pine forest nearby, wrapped about her and again for some reason she felt the momentary panic at his silent approach evaporate to be replaced with an immediate attraction.

Why this man? She'd done so well keeping her distance from everyone around her for five years. And now in a week's time she'd dreamed about Austin, fantasized what it would be like to be part of this family. Why?

Yes, he was capable of protecting her, at least that was the impression he gave her. Yes, he was appealing in a rugged way. And yes, he was loving and caring to his daughter and grandmother, watching over them.

But the real reason had to be because he was unattainable. She could admire him from a distance, but there would be no future for them. This attraction wouldn't lead to any kind of commitment. She wasn't good at commitments—the one serious relationship she'd had led to this situation. Hiding. Always on the run. Always looking over her shoulder.

No, Austin Taylor was safe to be attracted to. Nothing would come of it.

As she left the kitchen with Austin behind her, he flipped off the light, throwing the hallway into dimness. She paused a few seconds to allow her eyes to adjust. Her bedside lamp was on in her room and cast a soft glow out into the corridor at the other end. She headed toward it, every nerve ending pulsating with awareness of the man following her.

Near her bedroom she stopped and swung around to tell Austin goodnight. His gaze seized hers and held it. Intensity poured off him, raw, primitive for a few seconds before he managed to veil it.

"Are you and Misty going to the barn early tomorrow morning?"

"Probably, but not until after breakfast."

He stepped closer until half a foot separated them. "My grandmother was right about hiring you."

"What do you mean?" she asked, although her words came out in a breathless rush.

"I'll be perfectly honest with you. I didn't want to hire you. Too many questions. I was wrong. Obviously the answers weren't important. You're perfect for my daughter, and that's what is important." He leaned in a few inches. "And you're good for my grandma, too. That's a bonus."

The scent of his mint toothpaste teased her senses and alerted her cautious side. She should move back. And yet five years of staying back from others had made her so lonely. She'd always had a lot of friends in California. His very nearness prodded those yearnings to the foreground.

"Thank you, Hannah Williams, for taking the job." His whispered words caressed the corner of her mouth.

With supreme willpower she kept herself from melting against him, throwing her arms around him. Her lips tingled with the need to feel his against them.

It was too dangerous emotionally. She inched back, her fingernails digging into her palms. Because she couldn't do anything casually and walk away, she wanted it all. So it was okay to look but she could go no further.

Another step away. "I'll see you tomorrow."

His expression shadowed by the dim lighting, he glanced toward his daughter's bedroom then at Hannah. "Yes, tomorrow. Good night." Pivoting, he headed down the hallway.

Hannah escaped into her room and closed her door. She touched her mouth and wondered what his lips would feel like on hers.

Yeah, she was safe all right. Maybe from Devon Madison but not from Austin. How in the world had she thought he was safe to be attracted to because nothing would come of it? The thought of him chiseled a hairline crack in her heart she was afraid would only widen before she left the ranch.

FIVE

The next day the sun beat down on Hannah as she and Misty left the barn after spending some quality time with Candy, Barney and Snowball. The smile on the child's face rivaled the sun. Off in the distance, lodgepole pines poked up through the snow that covered the mountains, but in the valley most of the last snow had melted away to only a few patches in the shade.

"Daddy told me this morning it was gonna be warm today."

"He mentioned to me he's going to make time this afternoon to take us on a tour of the ranch."

"Me, too?"

"Yeah, especially you. I wouldn't want to see the Triple T without you to tell me about it."

The child's chest puffed out. "I can do that."

Out of the corner of her eye Hannah saw the cowhand who had been in the storage room heading straight for her. "Misty, you go on to the house. I'll catch up with you in a sec."

The fury on the man's face seemed to drop the temperature about her. She wouldn't let the child hear what she suspected was on the cowhand's mind. But as he neared, she braced herself for an onslaught. He stopped close to Hannah, near enough that she took a step back and her foot encountered one of the piles of snow still around.

He bent forward. "You had no right sticking your nose in my business." He tapped the side of his temple. "I'll remember you, little lady." With his breath reeking of tobacco, he spun on his booted heel and stomped away.

Flashes of Devon Madison's rage toward her after his brother's trial deluged her, holding her immobile as though she'd frozen in place. For a few seconds all Hannah could do was watch the man jump into his old, red pickup and screech out of the yard.

As he passed her on the road, paved around the house and barn area, she stepped back farther, seeing the anger in his expression. Both feet encountered the cold feel of snow as her tennis shoes sank into it.

Austin came out of the bunkhouse, probably drawn by the sound of the truck's tires burning rubber. He glimpsed her and advanced toward her. "Did he say or do something to you?"

"I—I..." She couldn't forget Devon's threats, ones that had set in motion what she'd done the past five years. That cowhand's pinpoint searing gaze had been so similar, even the same color—cold gray like the clouds of a blizzard.

Austin clasped her upper arm. "What did he do, Hannah?"

She swallowed the fear and looked at Austin. "He blames me for being fired."

"He blames you when..." His words splattered to a halt. He filled his lungs with gulps of air. "He's the one who I found taking a nap in the bunkhouse. He doesn't even stay here, but it was obvious he hadn't gotten much sleep over the weekend. I'd have fired him for that. That's the third time I've found him loafing on the job in the past month."

"That's not the way he sees it."

"I'm going into town the day after tomorrow. I'll find him and make him see the real reason. I thought I made myself clear. Obviously not."

The fact that Austin would do that surprised her because he was a busy man and tracking down the cowhand would take time away from his work and family. "Thanks, but just let it go. He'll calm down." At least she hoped he would. She'd seen to what lengths a person would go for revenge.

Austin removed his hat, raking his fingers through his hair and staring off into the distance toward the main road. "You're probably right. Besides, the reason I'm going into town is for Misty to see her pediatrician, and I want you to go, too. He wanted to see her after she'd been home a while to make sure she was doing okay."

"Sure. I'd love to see more of Sweet Creek." She started toward the front deck where Misty waited for her, her feet cold from the wet snow that had seeped inside her shoes.

"I figure you might be getting stir-crazy stuck on the ranch most of your time here."

She scanned the beauty surrounding her, meadows that in the spring would be littered with wildflowers, mountains not far away blanketed with a pristine cloak of snow, an occasional glimpse of a wild animal like a bighorn sheep or an elk. "Actually I love it here."

"The isolation doesn't get to you?" He tapped his cowboy hat against his jean-clad leg then put it back on.

"Isolation? There's Misty, Caroline, your employees

and you. That isn't isolation," she said above the chatter of a magpie in a nearby oak tree.

"That's how I feel, but my…" He snapped his mouth closed, his jaw set in a firm line.

"What?" she asked, aware she was probing into his personal life, but she wanted to know more about this man.

"My late wife hated it here. She always wanted to go to Billings or Missoula. She needed people—lots of people—around her. We weren't enough."

His last sentence, spoken with an edge of confusion and anger, tugged at her heart. "The grass is always greener on the other side of the fence?"

"Yes, although Jillian would never use those words. She'd thought she was marrying into a wealthy family that would allow her to move in a higher social class. Her words, not mine. We never have, and I wasn't going to start when my responsibilities are to the ranch and my family." At the bottom of the step, he lowered his head nearer her ear and whispered, "I haven't shared that with anyone else but my grandmother. I never want my daughter to know that side of her mother."

"I'd never say a thing to Misty. That wouldn't help her. She's already said something about her mother being gone for a long time."

"Thanks, I knew you wouldn't. I couldn't stand to listen to my daughter cry herself to sleep like she used to after one of Jillian's calls. Misty used to beg her mother to come home, but Jillian always had something she had to do and couldn't make it. Then she showed up unexpectedly. Misty was so excited."

"Daddy, are we gonna go now to see the ranch?"

He rotated toward his daughter, who had maneuvered

her wheelchair to the edge of the steps on the deck. He plastered a grin on his face, but Hannah saw the tic in his jaw as though at any moment the smile would collapse and his real feelings would push through.

"After lunch and a nap for you."

"But, Daddy, I don't need—"

"I want you rested when we go, munchkin. Okay?"

Misty nodded. "Hannah, can we eat now?"

Although she pretty well knew what time it was, Hannah made a production out of checking her watch. "It's only ten-thirty. Rene won't have it ready yet. Besides, weren't you going to write a thank-you note to the church for the wonderful party yesterday?"

"Oh, yes."

Hannah shared a glance with Austin, all strain in his expression gone. "Thanks for your help. I'm looking forward to the grand tour."

He chuckled. "I don't know how grand it will be. We'll be limited on where we can go. Now if I taught you to ride, you could go anywhere."

"Not in this lifetime," she said with a laugh and mounted the steps.

While Misty turned her wheelchair around and drove toward the front door, her father stood at the bottom of the stairs and said, "I can be mighty persuasive, ma'am."

When Hannah peered back at him, he winked and tipped his hat, then walked toward the barn.

In the large foyer Misty stopped, swinging about. "What did you and Daddy talk about?"

"You and our trip to the doctor in a few days."

A pout creased Misty's face. "I hate going to the doctor."

"Why, honey?" She knelt by Misty's wheelchair.

"It hurts."

"This should just be a checkup to make sure everything is going all right. I'll be there with you."

Her eyes brightened. "You will?"

"Yes. Now let's get that thank-you note written. You can tell me what to write and I will. We can mail it when we're in town."

Misty drove her wheelchair into the living room, where Caroline sat on the couch reading a book.

She looked up at her great-granddaughter and smiled. "Did you have a nice time at the barn?"

The little girl nodded. "Hannah, I have a picture I drew. I want to send it with the letter."

"Where is it? I'll get it."

"I can."

The whine of the wheelchair filled the quiet as Misty made her way from the room.

"She's already got an independent streak a mile wide, just like her daddy." Caroline closed her book.

"We can write the note in her bedroom or the kitchen."

"No, I'm at a good place in the story to stop. I'll be able to take it to my ladies group when we go into town on Wednesday. Austin's going to drop me off at church while Misty visits the doctor. This will be the first time I've been able to go in two months. I believe things are beginning to get back to normal."

"Yeah, normal," Hannah murmured, wishing her life was "normal." The nagging thought she needed to call Violet and find out why she was looking for her kept pestering her like a hungry mosquito.

"You could come with me to the meeting if you wanted."

Hannah shook her head. "I promised Misty I would be with her at the doctor's. I'm hoping that's okay with Austin. Do you think he'll mind?"

"No. He doesn't do well at the doctor's. You should see him when they had to give Misty a shot. His face went as white as newly fallen snow."

"Austin?"

"Tell you a secret. He hated shots as a child and has never grown out of that fear. When he was a little boy, he would hide when he knew he had to see the doctor. He even tried to keep any illness from his parents, just in case the doctor would want to give him a shot."

"He always seems so sure of himself."

"Oh, he is except for that. He knows what he wants and lets nothing stand in his way, but when he was Misty's age, he had to go through the series of rabies shots because a stray dog bit him. From then on he connected the doctor with getting a shot."

The image of him as a child, trying to be brave but not quite able to, firmed her growing attraction to the man because that was the way she felt most of time. She'd had her own phobia of shots as she grew up until she'd gotten over it when she had to have weekly allergy shots for several years. Because of the treatments, she'd conquered that fear enough to allow her now to do what she loved, help others, which sometimes meant giving shots. If she didn't have her job, she didn't know how she would make it through each day.

"Are you all right back there, Misty?" Austin asked as he steered the golf cart over a bumpy stretch of road.

"Yeah. Can we see Big Red?"

Hannah relished the fresh air. It had only a hint of a chill. She shifted around in the front seat and smiled at Austin's daughter, dressed in several layers. "Are you warm enough?"

She nodded, her cheeks rosy, her eyes bright with excitement.

"I'm glad the temperature is in the mid-fifties. Misty loves using the cart." He turned onto another gravel road, heading toward the mountains edging his property.

Austin slid his attention toward Hannah and hooked her gaze, reeling her in. An instant connection zipped between them, and she couldn't take her eyes off him.

For a few seconds she even forgot a five-year-old child was in the back until he said with a twinkle as though he knew exactly the effect he had on her equilibrium, "I've even let her steer the cart."

"I love that!" Misty piped in, her leg in the cast stretched out on the backseat and cushioned for the bumps.

"Isn't that dangerous?" Hannah dragged her gaze from Austin. If in this short amount of time he could throw her emotions into chaos, what was going to happen in a month? *Nothing. It can't because my life is a lie, and he'd never understand.* She had to remember that before she lost herself totally to his charm.

Austin chuckled. "She sits in my lap, and I control the speed, not that you can go too fast in one of these."

"Where are we going now?" Hannah asked, inhaling a deep breath of the pine-scented air, determined not to respond to the sound of his laugh.

"To see Big Red."

"Yippee!" Misty exclaimed.

"He's in the back pasture away from the mares and other male horses."

"By himself."

"Yeah, he's a stallion and doesn't tolerate other horses well."

"Why do you keep him?"

"Because he's a great stud."

"Like the bull you have in the pen by the barn?"

"Yes. See, you're getting the hang of all this."

"Hardly. About all I know is the difference between a horse and a cow."

"That's a start." He winked at her and brought the cart to a stop by a fenced pasture with one lone horse, a huge chestnut animal. "Will you unlatch the gate?"

"You're going to let him out?" Hannah gestured toward the stallion.

"No, we're going inside."

"Why? He doesn't play nice with others."

"Other horses, but he loves Misty, and I want my daughter to be able to pet him."

"Oh," Hannah murmured, slipped from the cart and strode toward the gate.

Big Red trotted toward her and stopped off to the side only a few feet away. Her eyes widened at the sight of how big he was. Maybe she should stay on this side of the fence. Don't animals smell fear?

With a quivering hand she raised the latch and pulled the gate toward her, only wide enough for Austin to drive the cart through. She quickly shut the gate, still standing outside the meadow.

When he parked, he rose and walked toward her. "C'mon. He won't bite. I promise."

"What about kicking me?"

"He only kicks other horses—usually of the male persuasion."

"Oh, that's reassuring." She eyed the stallion again. "Not!"

He opened the gate and held out his hand to her. "I'm not gonna let anything happen to you or Misty."

The little girl's giggles floated to her. She glanced at the child. Big Red bent his head toward Misty, and she patted the white stripe down his nose. If Austin's daughter wasn't afraid, why was she? She fit her hand in Austin's, the feel of his curling around her fingers causing her heartbeat to pick up speed. And it had nothing to do with fear.

"See how he is with Misty."

"He knows her. I'm a stranger."

"That's okay. I've got apple pieces, and he loves them."

"So you knew you were coming?"

"I know my daughter. Besides, I like to check on him. I've started expanding and breeding horses to sell. I've always wanted to do that rather than raise cattle, my father's preference. Big Red is an important part of that plan as I make the change over."

"Then move him closer to the house."

"He likes being alone."

Hannah tossed her head toward Big Red nuzzling Misty. "He does?"

Austin rubbed his hand on his chin. "You have a point, but I have to assure the safety of the other horses."

Austin let her set the pace. Hannah approached the stallion slowly, watching him closely interact with Misty. Like Candy, he seemed to realize she was hurt and wasn't her usual self. With each step that closed the distance between her and Big Red, she could see the draw. He was a magnificent example of a horse.

Within feet of the animal, he pulled his head away from Misty and turned it toward her, his big brown eyes locking on her. She gulped but stayed her ground. Austin released her grasp and went to the cart to retrieve the apple slices.

"Here, hold your hand out flat and give him this." He plunked a piece onto her palm.

With Austin next to her, Hannah straightened her arm toward the horse with her offering. Big Red moved several steps to her and plucked the treat from her. His nose tickled her skin, just like Candy's had with Misty.

"Here's another one."

Again she gave the stallion some apple. After he took it, intrigued at how gentle the horse had been, she asked, "Can I pet him?"

"He likes his neck scratched." Austin passed the rest of the apples to Misty. "Go ahead. Especially around his ears."

"Like my cat did. Okay." Cautiously, still not totally convinced she wouldn't end up hurt, she laid her palm on his neck, feeling the muscles beneath her hand.

After several strokes and a few scratches behind the ear, Hannah stepped away and stood next to Austin, allowing Big Red to return his attention to Misty, who happily fed him the rest of the slices.

"She loves living here." Hannah's gaze was fixed on the girl's face, and she remembered her own childhood, full of love and acceptance much like Misty's. She wanted to pass that along to her children. The thought came unbidden into her mind, and she sighed. It wasn't going to happen, but it was a nice dream.

"She was riding almost as soon as she could run around. If I let her, she'd live at the barn or in the pasture where I usually keep Candy most of the time."

"I know. I have a hard time keeping her in the house. I'm glad the weather has been better lately, but I also don't want her to tire herself out. That's when she seems to have the most problems with her breathing."

"We better head back. I don't want to tire her out, either."

"We haven't been out here that long." Hannah checked her watch. "Two hours! I can't believe it's been that long. Yeah, we'd better."

"Will you see to the gate?"

As Hannah ambled toward the fence, she surveyed the landscape around her. Gorgeous. A majestic beauty that proclaimed God's creation. Although she'd never been on a ranch for long and certainly not one this size, she'd discovered she'd been missing something. What would it be like to explore the nook and crannies of the Triple T?

When she was seated in the golf cart and Austin drove it back toward the main house, she glanced at Misty. The child had her head resting on her arm along the top of the backseat. Her eyes were opening and closing. "I think your daughter is more tired than she'll admit."

"When we get back, I'll carry her into the house and to her room. Will you get her wheelchair?"

"Yes." Hannah's gaze fell upon some horses in a pasture to the left. "And I think I'd like to take you up on the offer of a few riding lessons. That is, if you still want to teach me."

He shot her a look. "What changed your mind?"

"I love animals. How different can a horse really be?"

As he came to a stop under the carport at the front of the house, he laughed. "Believe me, a horse is different from a dog or a cat, but I think you'll do fine. Besides, I have the perfect mare for you. Sweet and docile."

"I like sweet and docile." Hannah followed Austin, who cradled Misty in his arms, his daughter's head pressed against his shoulder.

Inside the door she guided the electric wheelchair

toward the child's room a few paces behind Austin. When he placed her on her bed, Misty's eyes opened for a few seconds then immediately closed as she nuzzled into the covers.

Hannah tiptoed from the room with Austin exiting right after her. "Thank you for the grand tour."

"You're welcome. Now I need to get back to work. I have some calls to make in my office."

She watched him walk away, his long legs chewing up the distance quickly. He moved with an economical grace, no wasted motion. Once he'd accepted her presence on the ranch as Misty's health care provider, he'd become surprisingly warm and accommodating. Which was probably not good for her peace of mind. But she liked this Austin Taylor—a lot.

Hannah switched on the monitor in Misty's room in case the child had a problem. In the chair near the window, Hannah sat and pulled out her cell, punching in the number she'd found for Violet at the Missoula newspaper.

When the reporter came on the line, Hannah drew in a fortifying breath and asked, "Why are you looking for Jen Davis?"

"Is this Jen?"

Hannah glanced out the window at the meadow with horses grazing.

"Jen?"

The name brought back so many memories of when she was younger and more naïve. "Why are you looking for her?"

Violet sighed. "Because I think her life is in danger."

Hannah sat up straight, her back so rigid pain streaked down her spine. "Why do you think that?"

"You just need to be cautious."

"I'm— She always is. Again why should she be cautious?"

"Be careful about—" Violet paused, then finished with, "—your dealings with the U.S. Marshal's office."

"I don't have any—why?" Hannah wanted to protest she wasn't Jen Davis, but the denial wouldn't come out. There was no point in pretending she wasn't anymore.

"Because I think there's a leak in the U.S. Marshal's office or the FBI's."

"Why do you think that?"

"Because women with green eyes and in the Witness Protection Program in Montana are dying. There have been two murders so far. Both women are in a certain age range that you fit into."

"Why are they being killed?" Alarm roughened Hannah's voice.

"There's a hit out on Eloise Hill, who testified against a mobster in Chicago."

"But I'm not Eloise, and I've never been to Chicago."

"They don't know where she is so they are taking care of any woman in the program in Montana that fits the profile."

"They must really want this woman."

"Yes, it started in January with the murder of Ruby Maxwell then shortly after her Carlie Donald. Once they figured out what was going on, the U.S. Marshal's office has been looking for her."

"And you think a leak somewhere might be how the women are being tracked down?" Hannah leaned back, trying to ease the tension that gripped her body.

"Yes."

"Then calling the U.S. Marshal's office wouldn't be a wise move."

"Yeah, but I know that Micah McGraw, a deputy U.S. Marshal in the Billings office, is on the up-and-up. You can trust him. Please let him know where you are."

"Why should I? Didn't you say it was women in the program? I'm not in the program. Thank you for the information." Before Violet said anything else, Hannah clicked off, her hands shaking so badly the cell slipped from her fingers and landed in her lap.

Women being killed? A Chicago crime family? She was so thankful she'd dropped out of the Witness Protection Program two years before.

Suddenly a wheezing sound coming from the monitor sitting on her nightstand alerted Hannah that something was wrong with Misty. Hannah bolted to her feet, her cell crashing to the floor with a thud. As she rushed into the hallway, the sound grew louder and sent her heart pounding against her chest.

In Misty's doorway, Hannah's gaze riveted to the child on her bed, struggling to breathe, her face ashen, her eyes wide with fear. A tight cough racked Misty's body, and tears ran down her cheeks.

Hannah quickly went to the child's closet and retrieved her breathing machine, then plugged it in and sat on the bed to get Misty hooked up. "Honey, put this in your mouth," she said in a calm voice. "This will make you feel better."

Ten minutes into the treatment Austin showed up at the door. "Is she okay?"

"She'll be fine in a while."

Misty nodded slightly but kept drawing the mediated air into her lungs.

"I was heading out the back and thought I would check on her." He closed the space between them. "Maybe we overdid it today."

Misty's eyes grew round, and she took the tube out of her mouth. "No, I love it." A hint of red tinted her cheeks now.

Hannah directed the tube back to Misty's mouth. "She'll be back to her old self in no time."

"I see, but still, sweetheart, we'll need to be careful in the future not to do too much until you're recovered."

"I'm fine," she said, her words slurred by the plastic she still held in her mouth.

Hannah peered over her shoulder at Austin. "Go on to the barn. I've got everything under control. Once she's finished with her breathing treatment, I'm going to give her a sponge bath before dinner."

She'd known that would send Austin out the door with one last glance back at them on the bed. Hannah smiled.

In that instant he figured out she'd manipulated the situation and mumbled, "I'm gonna have fun when I get you on that horse."

The soft whine of Misty's wheelchair sounded in the silence of an early Sunday morning. A couple of yards from the barn, Hannah paused and slowly made a full circle, taking in the beauty of a new day. Hoar frost cloaked everything in tiny ice crystals. Some trees appeared as though snow caked their branches. A blanket of white masked the ground vegetation. This morning was colder than she thought. She and Misty wouldn't stay as long as usual.

"I left a note for your daddy on the kitchen table just in case he gets up and wonders where we are." Buttoning her heavy overcoat, Hannah entered the barn with Misty driving a little ahead of her toward Candy's stall.

Hannah glanced behind her at the rising sun, just

peeking over the horizon. She loved visiting all the animals and especially the mare that she'd had her first two riding lessons on. She was as sweet and docile as Austin had said.

She hurried ahead to open the stall door for Misty to go inside, then she entered, too, no longer afraid to shut them both in with the horse. A couple of barks resonated in the air. Barney. He'd be in here soon.

While the little girl gave Candy her treats for the day, Hannah thought back over the past few days. She was involved with the Taylor family more than an employee usually was. When she ate dinner with them all around the kitchen table, she felt a part of a group as she hadn't since she'd shared meals with her own family. She could grow used to that feeling of belonging. Its potency lured her into thinking everything was all right, that her life was typical and normal. Only when she went to bed at night did she get a reality check. She couldn't shake her nightmares even though she'd been at the ranch for nearly two weeks.

Why not?

That question nagged her in the morning, especially when no answer came to mind. Maybe the isolation, which she had thought would be a good thing. But she really didn't have a means of escape unless she stole a vehicle.

When she saw that they had been in the stall almost twenty minutes, Hannah stepped forward. "We probably better get the dog and cat food. Barney should be out there waiting for us. Even with us being early today, he tends to know when we are here."

"Can I brush Candy after that? I miss that."

Hannah peered from the small horse to Misty sitting in a wheelchair. "Yeah. We'll figure something out."

When Hannah opened the stall door, she half expected to see Barney sitting patiently for them a few feet away. Snowball ambled toward them but no Barney. She'd heard him earlier. Maybe he was out back.

"Wait. Let me check if he's behind the barn." While Snowball leaped into Misty's lap to be petted, Hannah strode toward the large double doors in the back nearer the bunkhouse. He often slept there.

As she neared the back exit, the scent of smoke teased her nostrils. Under the doors a gray haze seeped into the interior. She rushed forward and reached for the handle. Warm to the touch, she jerked her hand back. Swinging around, she hurried back to Misty, trying to school her features into a calmness she didn't feel.

"We need to get out of here. Hold on to Snowball."

The child lifted her head from cuddling it against the white cat and rotated her wheelchair around so she could head out the front. "What's wrong?"

"There's a fire."

Panic bolted through Hannah at the sight of the double doors that they'd come into the barn through and always left open, now shut. More smoke invaded the back of the barn.

Misty's eyes widened as she saw its insidious tentacles fan out. "Candy can't leave!" She swerved to the side and drove her chair toward the horse's stall.

"Go! Now!" All Hannah could remember was Austin telling her about the barn that had burned when he was a child, some animals dying in the fire, and the fact the structure was all wood.

Then the thought: was this the work of a hit man sent to take out another woman in the Witness Protection Program?

SIX

Frozen for a few precious seconds, Hannah couldn't shake the thought. She wasn't Eloise Hill and she wasn't involved with the program anymore. So how could an informant know she, Hannah Williams, was Jen Davis? It didn't make any sense. And if Violet was right and the U.S. Marshal's office with all its resources was looking for her and they hadn't found her, then she was safe from the phantom hit men.

Calm down. Think.

She stared behind her. No flames visible yet. But smoke continued to ooze under the double doors at the back. She waved her arms. "Come on. Go!"

Tears streaked down the child's face. "But, Candy—"

"You keep going. I'll get her. Don't wait for me. Get outside." Hannah watched the child drive toward the front and prayed to the Lord that way wasn't blocked or they were truly trapped.

Misty stopped and glanced back. "I'm going. Go ahead."

After making sure the child was clear and out of harm's way, Hannah raced to the stall and thrust the door open. The horse charged out, nearly knocking Hannah to the ground. The mare's eyes wide with fright, she bolted toward the one double door Misty had disappeared through.

The scent of smoke grew stronger. Hannah heard the whinnies of the other horses locked in their stalls. The sound of hooves striking the wooden doors drowned out the hammering of her heartbeat. She peered back at the thickening smoke and made a decision. There was still a little time to save some of the animals, if not all.

Covering her mouth and nose with the bottom of her sweatshirt, she ran to each stall she could get to and threw open its door, making sure this time she was well out of the way of the terrified animal as it stampeded toward freedom.

She'd left the stalls near the front until last. She thrust two more open, then turned to the last one by the barn entrance. She could get to it on her way out.

This last one, Lord, then I'll leave.

As she neared the stall, the noise from inside as the horse's hooves came down on the door underscored how panicked the usually docile mare was. She was only a few feet from being able to release the latch when the door crashed open and the horse careened out of her prison and straight for Hannah, who stood between the mare and her escape.

Hannah tried to move but the thousand-pound animal barreled into her, clipping her on the shoulder, which sent Hannah flying to the ground. The hard impact propelled all the air from her lungs. The smoke continued to roll toward her.

The scent of coffee laced the air, drawing Austin toward the kitchen. Hannah must have fixed it. She'd been preparing it most mornings this week. She rose earlier than even he did.

When he entered, his gaze swept the room. Where was she?

Austin spied the note on the kitchen table as he crossed to the sink to fill a mug. Changing his course, he snatched up the paper and read where Hannah and his daughter were so early in the morning. He glanced at the time and decided to go to the barn. Back at the counter, he poured himself some dark brew, then walked toward the front of the house.

As he emerged onto the deck, he caught a whiff of the smell. Smoke. His attention flew toward the barn as he set his mug down on the railing, then practically leaped from the top step to the ground at the sight of Misty coming out of the front entrance with Candy almost running over her. He zeroed in on the structure. From the back a mushrooming cloud of smoke roiled upward toward the sky, being chased by flames.

As he ran, he fished for his cell and put in a call to the volunteer fire department fifteen minutes away. More horses shot out of the entrance, galloping in all directions.

He pinned Misty with a look. "Are you okay?"

"Yes, but Hannah's inside."

Near the barn he pressed the alarm, a high-pitched siren blasting the air.

He turned back to Misty. "Go to the house. Get Granny. You stay there. I'll get Hannah."

As he started into the barn, he glimpsed his daughter heading away. At the entrance a mare shot out of the door, nearly knocking him down. He removed his jacket and put it to his mouth and nose, then ran low farther into the building.

"Hannah!"

Lord, help me find her.

He scanned the area; the growing smoke inside stung his eyes. Then he saw her nearby, only a few feet from the doors, crumpled on the earthen floor. For a second his heartbeat felt like it had skidded to a halt.

When he saw her move, trying to rise, he nearly collapsed with relief.

Quickly he knelt and scooped her up. A crack at the back of the barn followed by a flaming timber from the wall plunging to the ground underscored the danger. The earth beneath his knees shook. He surged to his feet and raced out the door. Another crash and boom propelled him to go faster across the yard.

In the open he staggered to a safe distance, coughing, trying to hold on to Hannah. He managed to place her on the frost-covered ground as more coughs racked him.

He prayed the volunteer firemen would be here soon. In the meantime, his own cowhands used what firefighting equipment they had to protect the surrounding structure so the fire didn't spread. The barn would be gone. There would be nothing they could do to save it even if it would take hours to completely burn.

"Misty, okay?" she rasped, then starting coughing.

"She's fine. I'm taking you to the small hospital in Sweet Creek. They may have to transport you to Missoula."

"I'll be okay." She struggled to prop herself on her elbows, swayed and crumbled back to the ground.

"Yeah, I see that." His throat burned as though the fire rampaged through him. "As soon as the fire department gets here and you can get some oxygen, we're leaving." His men and the volunteer firefighters would take care of containing the fire only to the barn.

"You can't." She waved her hand toward the blaze. "You need to be here." Again she began hacking, tears glistening in her eyes.

He thrust his face close, blocking her view of the fire. "You come first."

You come first. Those words had flirted with Hannah's emotions the whole time she was being checked out by the doctor at the hospital and being given the okay to go home. And on the trip back to the ranch in the late afternoon, they still played around in her mind, as if she were participating in a hide-and-seek game. How could she be falling for Austin? She always guarded her heart so well. She knew a relationship between them was doomed from the beginning.

She closed her eyes and laid her head against the seat in Austin's SUV. Her throat and lungs burned. Her head pounded. The stench of smoke still clung to her. But she was alive, and Misty was all right. The Lord had answered her prayer, and that comforted her. He hadn't totally given up on her.

Austin made a turn. She inched one eyelid up to see where they were. A sigh escaped her lips. The ranch. Home—but only for a short time. If only it wasn't.

"Are you sure you're all right?" Austin's question, his voice as raspy as hers from the smoke, made her open her eyes.

"You heard the doctor. My tests came back normal. No permanent damage. We both needed to get ho—back to the ranch." The ranch wasn't her home, would never be.

"My foreman assures me he's taken care of everything. Max has been with me for a long time and I trust his word. He had to run the ranch while I was with Misty in Missoula."

"I'm glad you can trust him." She didn't know what trust meant anymore, although she could see herself trusting Austin. He was that kind of man.

"Yeah. But obviously there's someone out there who has a grudge against me. Max told me the fire chief found empty cans of gasoline behind the barn. He thinks whoever set the fire soaked the whole lower backside of the barn so it would burn fast and there would be no way to save it or the animals in it." He slanted a look toward her. "But you saved them. You shouldn't have risked it."

"I promised Misty I would get Candy. Then after that I was going to leave but couldn't bear hearing the horses in their stalls, trapped. I had to do something."

"And you could have died."

"Have I thanked you in the past hour for coming in and getting me?"

"We could trade thank-yous all day. You saved my daughter, and there are no words I could say that would adequately express my gratitude for that."

As Austin crested the rise near the main house, Hannah straightened and braced herself for the sight before her. The hired hands and fire department had stopped the fire from spreading to the bunkhouse and other structures, but what little remained of the barn lay in a smoldering shambles of burnt timbers and ashes.

"Did they find all the horses? Candy?"

"All but one. A few of the guys are out looking for the last one. And Candy is fine. Max says he let Misty love on her for a while, and the mare calmed right down."

"How's Misty taking it?"

"She didn't say much other than to make sure you were all right. She made me say that several times as though she didn't believe me the first two times. The last time I called Granny said she was taking a nap, a long one."

"She's emotionally exhausted. I'll go see her right away."

Austin parked in front of the main house and angled toward her. "And you aren't exhausted? I know I can't keep you from checking on Misty, but then go rest, take your own long nap. Granny and I will take care of Misty."

You come first. Those words rang in her mind yet again. "But you've got to have so much to do right now."

"Which I'll get done, but I have good people working for me." He captured her gaze and her hand lying on the seat between them. "Do I have to escort you to your room to make sure you follow my or—suggestion?"

She laughed. "Nice save. No, I'll pop in and see if Misty is up and check on her, then go take a nap. Okay?"

"Perfect."

The smile he gave her encompassed his whole face down to the twinkle in his eye that warmed her. She opened the door.

"I'll be at what's left of the barn for a while, then I'm going to have to make some calls to house some of my horses until I can get my main barn rebuilt."

She climbed from the Jeep and mounted the steps to the deck. Caroline threw open the front door before she had a chance to ring the bell. Her smile of welcome matched her grandson's.

"You should have stayed at the hospital overnight."

"And gone stir-crazy. No, Caroline. I'm fine. I spent some time on oxygen and they gave me some medication. My lungs feel a whole lot better than they did. Time will heal me."

"I've heard doctors can make the worst patients, but I

think that extends to anyone in the medical field," the older woman said with a chuckle.

She didn't think she'd be able to get the picture of the flames and smoke out of her mind any time soon, but she would at least rest.

Caroline tsked. "I'm surrounded by stubborn people. I'll be in the living room if you need me."

Hannah headed straight for Misty's room and peeked inside. The little girl whimpered although she was still asleep and tried to turn over but couldn't because of the cast. Hannah covered the distance to the bed as quickly as she could. The child settled back into the covers, her eyes closed. The frown that puckered her brow smoothed out, and Misty relaxed back into a calm sleep.

Hannah itched to brush the girl's long black hair away from her face and from around her neck, to reassure herself the child was truly all right, but she was afraid that would awaken Misty. Today had been traumatic, and she needed her rest. But she wanted to hold the child and hug her for as long as she would allow her.

The thought of how this morning could have ended inundated her. A shudder wiggled down Hannah's length.

Thank You, Lord, for answering my prayer. I don't know what I would have done if Misty had been hurt further.

Hannah left the child sleeping and entered her own room, the bed beckoning. After stretching out on the coverlet, she closed her eyes and tried to quiet the unrest and questions starting to fly around in her brain. Who wanted to set fire to the barn? Was there any way it could have been connected to her being here? In her gut she didn't think so. Mainly because whoever came after her would need to make sure she died. That person would want to do it personally to assure the job was done. She knew Devon Madison well enough to realize he would expect that from any thug he sent to kill her. And the same for a hit man after Eloise Hill. Setting a fire wasn't her idea of a professional hit.

Which left what Austin thought: someone had a grudge against him. The first and only person was Bob Douglas, the man fired the week before. His threat resounded in her mind. *I'll remember you, little lady.* And his tone and look had definitely conveyed not in a nice way.

Would he risk killing Misty to get at her? That didn't really make sense to her. He was mad and might hurt her, but he didn't feel like a cold-blooded murderer—at least of human beings. But animals? Maybe. She and Misty didn't normally go to the barn that early. No one was usually around at that time, especially on a Sunday. So whoever set the fire was probably trying to destroy the barn and the animals in it.

She turned over and tried to blank her mind. She couldn't. Some shadowy nemesis gripped it, and that was all she could think about. Giving up on resting, she swung her feet to the floor and rose. After checking on Misty again, she ambled toward the living room.

Several masculine voices alerted her to the fact the Taylors had visitors. She almost turned around to go back to her room, then decided she couldn't take the solitude. Pausing in the entrance into the living room, she scanned the faces of the people sitting. Two men in uniform had joined Caroline and Austin.

Austin glimpsed her and shoved to his feet. "Sheriff, this is Hannah Williams. She was with Misty in the barn when it caught fire."

The lean, medium tall man with his tan cowboy hat in

his hand stood as well as the other male with him. The craggy-faced sheriff nodded toward her. "I'm sure glad you and Misty got out alive, ma'am. This is Deputy Collins. We're here to get statements from everyone. After talking to the fire chief, there's no doubt this was arson. Nothing accidental about all that gasoline."

Hannah crossed the space and took a chair across from the sheriff. "I'll help any way I can. Anyone who would set a fire knowing animals were inside makes me sick." The sound of the horses' fear echoed through her mind, and she shivered. "I want him brought to justice."

"My thoughts exactly. And I aim to do that, ma'am. Did you see or hear anything?"

"No, Misty and I were in Candy's stall. I didn't see the smoke until we left to go feed Snowball and Barney." She snapped her fingers. "Yes, I did. I'm not sure how important this is, but I did hear Barney bark a couple of times then he was quiet. I was surprised he wasn't in the barn like Snowball was. We usually feed the pets a couple of hours later, but he starts hanging around early like the cat."

"We haven't found Barney," Austin said, his voice tight.

Her gaze connected with his. "He's missing?" Fear rose to the surface. "You think the person did something to the dog?" She prayed that wasn't the case. Misty loved that dog.

Austin drew in a shaky breath. "I hope not. That's Misty's dog and…"

"I understand some of the men are combing the area from the barn outward. There's still a horse missing as well as Barney," the sheriff said to fill the silence left by Austin.

"How do you know how many horses made it out of

the barn? I didn't even think to count them." She thought back to the frantic scene in the barn, rubbing her temple. "I think I let all of them out of their stalls."

Austin cleared his throat. "Misty counted them as they came out."

Hannah smiled. "You've got one smart daughter."

He shared a brief grin with her, the corners of his mouth quivering. "Yeah, I think so, but then fathers usually do."

"So other than hearing Barney barking that's all you can think of?" The sheriff ran his fingers along the brim of his hat, rotating it in his hand.

"Sorry. I wish I had more. When Misty and I went to the barn, I didn't see anything. Do you suspect anyone?"

"Right before you came in, Austin and I were talking about who might have a grudge against him. He gave me a couple of names I'll be checking out."

"Bob Douglas?" She glanced toward Austin.

He nodded. "As well as Kenny Adams and Slim Miller."

"Who are they?" Her muscles aching from holding herself so rigid, Hannah finally relaxed against the back cushion.

"Two men who are still in the area that I had to fire in the past year."

"Ms. Williams, why did you ask if it was Bob Douglas? What made you say him besides the fact that Austin fired him?"

"A week ago I found him in the storage room trying to get rid of a cigarette butt. The place smelled of smoke. I'm sure he'd been smoking in there. I figured someone who got rid of cigarettes irresponsibly might have used fire to get back at Austin for letting him go."

The sheriff shifted his attention to Austin. "You told me you fired him because he was lazy."

"Yeah, ultimately that was the reason. That and the fact he lied to me about smoking when I asked him point-blank about it."

The sheriff stood. "I'll check him out first. Even pay him a little visit today. He was the most recent person fired."

Austin walked with the two lawmen toward the foyer. "I know you don't have to keep me in the loop, but I sure would appreciate it if you would let me know how the investigation is going."

"Will do." The sheriff paused in the doorway, put his hat back on and tipped it toward Caroline. "Nice seeing you, Caroline. You just keep getting younger and younger." While Austin's grandmother blushed, the lawman swiveled his gaze to Hannah. "Ma'am, if you think of anything else, call me."

"I will."

Hannah released a long breath as the sound of the front door closing drifted to her. "How long has Misty been sleeping?"

Caroline looked at her watch. "Three hours."

"Good. She didn't sleep well last night, and then with all that's happened, she needs the rest."

Austin started to come back into the living room, but a knock at the front door drew him away. A few minutes later Austin finally entered the room. "They found the mare and are checking her out then putting her in the south pasture."

"But no Barney?" Hannah asked, restless energy surging through her. She rose, needing to move around.

"One team still hasn't returned. There's hope."

Please, Lord, bring Barney home. If anything happened to Barney, it would break Misty's heart. It would break her heart, too, Hannah thought, having become fond of the dog in the past two weeks.

"I'm gonna be near the barn, supervising the relocation of the some of the horses if you need me for anything."

"I'm going to check on Misty. Can I get you anything, Caroline?" Hannah said as Austin strode into the foyer.

She waved her hand. "No, I'm fine. Go, take care of Misty, and if she's still sleeping, relax."

Out in the entry Hannah stopped Austin. "If Misty is still sleeping, is it okay if I use your computer in your office?"

"Sure," he said, thrusting open the front door and leaving.

After checking on Misty, who was still sleeping, Hannah made her way to Austin's office. She would do some surfing on the Internet to see if she could find out anything first on Ruby Maxwell or Carlie Donald. She wouldn't have much time, but she was too wound right now to relax.

Fifteen minutes later, she discovered the write-up on a Ruby Maxwell's funeral. But no mention of the woman being murdered. Then she looked for anything on Carlie Donald. Nothing but a funeral notice. If the women were murdered, wouldn't something be in the news about the killings? She'd wanted to know the facts around these so-called professional hits. She just didn't know what to make of it all. She certainly didn't have any connections to a Chicago crime family.

Did Violet Kramer know what she was talking about? What if the reporter was looking for a story where there wasn't a story? Hannah glanced at the clock on Austin's desk and noticed the time. She would have to research

Eloise Hill later when she got another chance to use Austin's computer, but she was beginning to believe the reporter was reading more into the situation than what was really going on. She quickly left the office to check again on Misty.

When Hannah eased Misty's bedroom door open all the way, a smile spread across the little girl's face. "You're okay." She pushed herself up to a sitting position.

"Yep, nothing gets me down for long. Kinda like you."

The grin grew even wider. "Thanks for saving Candy. She's so special to me."

"You're welcome." Hannah sat on the bed. "So how do you feel?"

"Okay." Her mouth turned down.

"Are you sure about that? You aren't sounding very convincing."

The child peered down at her hand clutching the coverlet. "It was scary. All that smoke. The flames." She stared up into Hannah's gaze. "Somethin' coulda happened to you."

"Yeah, but the Lord was looking out for you and me."

"And Candy and Snowball." Her eyebrows scrunched together. "Where was Barney?"

"He wasn't in the barn. I think the fire scared him like the horses. They're still rounding up all the animals."

"I wanted to run away, too. I couldn't. You were inside. I was scared."

Hannah scooted back against the headboard next to Misty and wound her arm about the child's shoulders. "I know the feeling. You were so brave today, Misty. I'm all right."

Silence hung between them for a moment, Misty laying her head against Hannah. "I had a hard time holding Snowball. He kept wiggling."

"He was scared, too." Hannah stroked her hand down Misty's arm, wishing she could take the girl's fears away. She'd had two near-death experiences in a couple of months. That was a lot to handle as an adult, let alone a child. "It's okay to feel scared. When you get that way, it's good to talk about it with someone like your daddy."

"Or you."

"You can tell me anything."

"I didn't want anything to happen to you," Misty stumbled to a halt for a few seconds, then added, "like Mommy."

Her throat tight, Hannah pressed the girl closer. "Nothing's going to happen to me, Misty." Maybe when she left the ranch, she could at least call and talk to Misty occasionally or e-mail her.

Austin appeared in the doorway, a grim expression on his face that he immediately wiped away when Misty glimpsed him.

"Daddy!"

"Hi, munchkin. I'm sorry I haven't had much time to be with you." He closed the space to the bed, leaned down and kissed his daughter on the cheek. "Are you okay?"

Misty nodded, her smile in place.

"Good. I need to see Hannah for a minute. I'm still seeing to all the animals, but we'll talk later. She'll be right back in." Austin took Hannah's hand and drew her toward the hallway.

A few feet from Misty's door, he turned toward Hannah and stepped close. "They found Barney."

"Dead?" she asked, remembering his earlier grim expression.

The same one descended. "He's barely alive. I think he was poisoned. There was a half-eaten steak nearby. They found him under a thick set of bushes behind the bunkhouse. I wanted you to know before I leave. I'm taking him to the vet. I don't want Misty to know until we know if he's gonna make it or not."

She squeezed his hand. "I'm so sorry. They have to find the person who did this."

"I'll be posting a couple of guards around this area until he's caught. I won't have a repeat of the fire this morning." The hard line of his jaw and the glint in his eyes attested to his fierce determination to make sure that didn't happen.

"Go. I'll take care of Misty. We'll have so much fun she won't have time to think about what happened today or about Barney."

"Thanks." He sent her a half grin as he pivoted and strode away.

Hannah heaved a deep sigh, the day suddenly swamping her as though her body finally realized all it had exactly been through. But at the moment it didn't make any difference how tired she was. She needed to take care of Misty. Make her feel safe and loved.

Exhausted, Hannah settled more comfortably onto the couch in the living room where she could see when Austin came into the house from the vet's. She didn't want to go to sleep until she knew what happened to Barney. An hour ago Caroline had finally gone to bed, no longer able to keep herself awake. Misty went to sleep much earlier, still tired even after the long nap.

The quiet of the house, the room only lit by one lamp in the corner, lured Hannah into a semi-awake state. The silence like a balm surrounded her in solace, and she couldn't resist surrendering to it…

The next thing she knew Austin hovered over her, shaking her shoulder gently. "Hannah, are you all right?"

Seeing the worry in his eyes, she gave him a smile. "I'm fine." She unfolded her legs and placed her feet on the floor, straightening. "How's Barney?"

"He's gonna make it. At least that's what the doc thinks. He finally sent me home and told me he'll know for sure tomorrow morning and call me."

Relief trembled through her. "I'm so glad. I won't say anything to Misty but let you talk with her about what happened to Barney. She's going to want to see all the animals tomorrow the second she wakes up."

"Ask her to wait. Candy and the mare you rode are going to be kept in a pasture close to the house. That way they'll be more accessible for you two." He eased down next to her on the couch. "Most of my horses aren't stabled. I sometimes keep a few in the barn for pleasure riding. Usually only the sick ones or a mare about to give birth. I hate keeping them confined too long. Even Candy is usually in a field except lately because of Misty's injuries."

"I'll keep Misty here until you've talked with her."

"Did you get any rest?"

"Not much."

In one fluid motion he rose and offered her his hand. "C'mon. I'll walk you to your door."

Wrapping her fingers around his, she let him tug her up flat against him. She clasped one upper arm while for a few seconds her body pressed against his. The feel of the semi-embrace felt so right she wanted to explore the sensations his nearness stirred in her. She peered up into his dark coffee-colored eyes, held captive by their swirling depths. She swallowed several times to ease the tightness in her throat but nothing helped.

In the dimness, he reached up and smoothed her hair

back from her face, then framed it. "I don't know what I would have done without you today. There aren't words to express my thanks."

"I did what anyone would have done."

"Don't sell yourself short. But if there is ever a next time, and I pray to God there isn't, don't put your life on the line for my animals. You came close to dying today, Hannah, and I wouldn't have been able to live with that. Promise me you won't."

She covered his hands on her face. "I can't do that. Besides, why are we talking about next time? How often do barns burn down around here?" She tried to inject humor into the last question, but the expression on his face remained serious.

"I'm hoping never again. Promise me you won't take unnecessary risks."

Urgency and care sounded in his voice. She couldn't ignore it. "I promise I won't." She would only be here another five or six weeks anyway. He didn't need to know her whole life was a risk—that she had a death warrant hanging over her head.

The tension beneath her palms and in his body melted, and he exhaled a deep breath. "Thanks. Now let me see you to your room before you fall asleep on your feet. I don't think you're gonna need warm milk tonight." He settled his arm over her shoulder and cradled her in the crook of his arm.

"I don't think so, either." She cushioned her head against him, his male scent enveloping her.

"I'll check on Misty and take her monitor so if something happens in the middle of the night I can take care of it."

"But that's my job."

"No, I'm her father. It's my job and you need to get a good night's sleep."

At her door she tilted her head up to argue with him, but the words died in her throat. The simmering look in his eyes robbed her of all coherent thought. She should draw back. But she wanted him to kiss her, had for days.

Slowly he leaned down until his mouth was only inches from hers.

SEVEN

Austin settled his mouth on hers, wrapping his arms around her and dragging her to him. Pressed against him, she surrendered to the kiss, and for a moment she reveled in the feel of being in his embrace.

When his lips left hers, he rested his forehead against hers, cupping her face. "I've wanted to do that since that first night we had warm milk together."

The feel of his palms against her cheeks, the tingle of her mouth where his had been, the minty taste of him on her lips, the thundering of her heartbeat in her ears overwhelmed her senses. She slid her eyes closed to block his appealing features from her view, but his image imprinted itself in her mind. The connection between them was strong. He made her believe in tomorrows. He gave her hope.

And she knew there was no hope for them.

Hannah finally stepped away, his arms falling to his sides. "I'd better get that monitor for you." Quickly she escaped into her bedroom, retrieved the piece of equipment and returned to the hall.

Austin stood where she'd left him, no emotion on his face. She thrust the monitor toward him, keeping herself at arm's length. After he took it, she spun on her heel and covered the few feet to her door.

Pausing, she glanced back, hating the sudden wall between them, put there by her. "For the record, I've wanted you to kiss me, too." Then she disappeared into her room and closed the door before she threw herself into his arms.

A scream pierced through the dark wall of Hannah's dreamless sleep, pulling her toward wakefulness. Still exhausted, she snuggled deeper into her covers, resisting. Quiet lured her back to the floating blackness. When she was close to surrendering totally again, the sound of sobbing intruded.

Misty!

Hannah popped up in bed and scanned the darkened room, listening. A shaft of light from the hallway drew her attention. She placed her feet on the floor and grabbed her robe, belting it as she moved toward the hall. Although Austin had the monitor to listen if Misty had problems, she'd decided to leave her door ajar anyway. Just in case the child needed her.

In the corridor a flood of light came from Misty's room. She hurried inside and found Austin sitting on his daughter's bed, hugging the child to him while she cried, loud heart-wrenching sobs that tore at Hannah's fragile composure. She moved forward, needing to help the girl.

She placed a hand on Austin's shoulder. He was still dressed in his jeans and long-sleeved blue shirt from earlier. "What can I do?"

"She had a nightmare about the fire." Austin stroked his daughter's back. "Honey, you're safe. You're here with me—and Hannah. Nothing is gonna happen to you."

"It was—" the child hiccupped "—scary."

"I know, baby. But you're all right now. Safe. In your bed." His soothing, calm words murmured over and over finally eased the tears.

Misty leaned back. "I almost lost Snowball. He wouldn't stay still."

Austin took his daughter's face between his hands while his thumbs wiped away the wet tracks on her cheeks. "He's fine. And see Hannah is, too."

Hannah came forward and sat next to Austin, touching the child's arm. "We'll visit Candy as soon as your father says we can."

"Tomorrow, honey. I've got her in a nearby pasture. I'll bring her to you. First thing so you don't have to fret. She's okay, though."

"Barney?"

Austin shot Hannah a look, full of worry. A silent question entered his gaze. Should he say anything about the dog now? Misty was a tough little girl. She nodded once.

"Barney's at the vet. He ate something that didn't agree with him, but the vet thinks he'll be fine."

Misty's eyes widened. "He was hurt."

"Not in the fire, honey. He got hold of a bad piece of meat. Hopefully I'll be able to pick him up tomorrow."

"We didn't get to feed him. I forgot when the fire…" Tears returned to pool in Misty's eyes.

Austin clasped Misty's arms and waited until he had her full attention before saying, "You are *not* to blame for him eating the meat because you didn't get to feed him. It happened at the time of the fire, maybe before."

"Sweetie, that was why he wasn't there with Snowball."

Misty yawned.

"Honey, why don't you lie down and try to sleep?" Austin helped his daughter get back under the covers.

However, doubt clouded the little girl's eyes.

"Tell you what, Misty. Why don't I stay with you until you get to sleep?" Hannah tucked her in, not meeting Austin's gaze. Being with the little girl was more for herself than the child. She needed to feel she was helping Misty. Her wellness, physically and emotionally, had become important to Hannah.

Misty's eyelids drooped. "That would be great." Another yawn escaped her as she cuddled under the warmth of the coverlet.

Hannah stood to move around to the other side of the bed, still not wanting to look at Austin. She knew she should be resting, that tomorrow would be a long day, but Misty came first, not only for Austin, but for her as well.

Austin rose, too, bending close to her ear and whispering, "I can stay. You don't need to do that. You should get your sleep."

She turned, his face so near she could lean forward a few inches and kiss his mouth. And she wanted to. That thought sent her heartbeat spinning out of control and for a few seconds throwing her off kilter. Finally blinking to break his visual hold, she averted her gaze. "I wouldn't sleep much for worrying about Misty. This way I'll be able to rest," she replied in a low voice.

"Fine. But go back to bed when she falls to sleep. I still have the monitor so I can be back if I need to." Angling away from her, Austin leaned over Misty and kissed her cheek. "Good night, honey."

"Night, Daddy," she mumbled, her eyes opening then immediately closing.

Hannah waited until Austin left before slipping onto the bed next to Misty, curling on her side to face the child.

Misty turned her head toward her. "Night, Hannah. I'm glad you're here."

"Me, too."

The child grinned, but it almost instantly faded as her eyes fell closed.

But the smile stayed with Hannah, warming a cold place in her heart that had been there since she'd left California and been thrust into a life she'd never wanted. She closed her own eyes and for a while she could visualize Misty as her daughter—and Austin as her husband.

Austin rode across the meadow to check on the horses in the old barn before bringing Candy to the house. The sun sneaked above the tree line to the east, the ribbons of pink and orange beginning to vanish. A stillness hung in the cool air, no longer laced with the scent of burning wood.

On his way out of the house this morning, he'd stopped by his daughter's room to check on her. To his surprise he'd found not only Misty but Hannah, sleeping soundly. His child had been huddled up against Hannah with the woman's arm cushioning his little girl. The sight had stolen his breath. His wife had never done that, and the fact that Hannah had awed him. She had gone above and beyond the boundaries of her job description. Every barrier he had tried to erect against caring for Hannah was quickly coming down.

This certainly wasn't the best time to pursue a romantic relationship. His track record didn't give him a lot of confidence. But that kiss last night had rocked him. He couldn't deny her effect on him any longer. He cared about her deeply, and he wanted to explore where this would take them.

As he neared Big Red's pasture, he searched for the stallion. But all that greeted him was an empty field. When he saw the gate standing wide open, he grew cold. The latch didn't open easily. The only way would be by a person's hand. The cold chill spread throughout him the closer he came to the meadow.

Someone had let him out on purpose.

Probably the same person who had set his barn on fire.

At the gate he closed it, then climbed the fence to survey the area one more time before sounding the alarm. No Big Red. When he jumped back to the ground, he investigated the earth around him to see if the person had used a vehicle, but there weren't any tire tracks visible in the dirt.

Not only was Big Red an expensive stallion and valuable stud, but a loose Big Red could cause damage and trouble. And whoever let him out knew that.

"This is delicious, Caroline." Hannah took another bite of the Southwestern omelet Austin's grandmother had fixed.

Misty gulped down the rest of her milk. "Can I have more toast?"

"You sure can." Caroline popped two pieces of bread into the toaster. "With butter and strawberry jam, no doubt."

"Yep."

Hannah reached over and wiped the milk moustache from the child's upper lip. "Why don't you sit down and let me finish up for you, Caroline?"

"No, this is my treat. I don't cook like I used to since

Rene came to work for us, but she's helping down at the bunkhouse with the men who are here to start the cleanup. Besides, my omelet is still cooking." When the older woman took the toast and buttered each slice, she sighed. "I used to eat several pieces at breakfast but those days are over since I began counting my carbs."

"Carbs? What's that?" Misty snatched one slice of toast as Caroline put the plate on the table.

"Something this old lady can't have too much of."

"It's things like breads." The sound of the back door opening pulled Hannah's gaze toward it.

The severe expression on Austin's face didn't bode well. Was it Barney? Had he heard from the vet? He peered at his daughter, his features transforming into a neutral countenance.

Misty brightened, a grin spreading from ear to ear. "You have Candy?"

"Yes. Let me check on something then eat before I take you to her." Austin crossed the kitchen and left.

Hannah scooted back her chair. "I'll be back in a sec."

She hurried after him, catching up with him right before going into his office. "What's happened? Is it Barney?"

He shook his head, the tension returning to his expression. "The vet called, and I'll be able to pick him up later today. It's Big Red. He's missing."

"Missing? What do you— Oh, no. The arsonist took him?"

"That's what I'm thinking, or he's loose somewhere on the ranch. I sent a couple of search parties out to cover the property. I'll join them after the sheriff comes."

"Can I help by picking up Barney for you? I figure you'll be busy."

"You don't know the area."

"Maybe Caroline and Misty can go with me. We'll make it an outing. Misty will think it's a treat."

"Fine. Getting her away from the ranch while we hunt for Big Red might be for the best." He raked his hand through his hair. "Frankly I'm worried about what I'll find when we do locate him."

"You think the guy killed the stallion?"

"He didn't think twice about burning down a barn with horses in it. I do know one thing. I won't rest until I discover who this man is." His fierce tone emphasized his determination to bring the perpetrator to justice.

She wanted to erase the dark shadows from beneath his eyes, to wipe the exhaustion that gripped Austin. The past twenty-four hours had been a nightmare for him. Having someone after him was something she could relate to.

She reached out and touched his arm. "I'll help you any way I can. Don't worry about Barney. We'll take care of the dog."

"Is Misty finally asleep?" Caroline asked, folding the newspaper and putting it on the coffee table in front of her.

"Yeah. I stayed with her until she nodded off." Hannah eased down on the couch next to Caroline, setting the monitor next to the newspaper.

The headline of a story in the *Missoula Daily News* caught Hannah's attention about a woman murdered. The byline was the same reporter that Saul had talked about a couple of weeks ago. Violet Kramer.

Hannah picked up the paper and scanned the story. Quinn Smith allegedly murdered a woman for trying to do the right thing—expose a murder and bring the guilty to justice. Hannah's heart went out to the woman who had died. She'd done the same thing. She'd done what was right, testify against Cullen for killing a man. Would she end up murdered like Lisa? She shivered at the thought.

"I see you're reading the story Violet wrote. I met her while I was in Missoula. She was doing a piece on the hospital foundation. I know someone on the board, and she introduced me when Violet was at the hospital interviewing her."

"When Misty was staying there?"

"Yes. I follow what she writes now. She's very resourceful and determined. I liked her."

Hannah stiffened, turning her head away. She didn't want Caroline to see the fear that was probably evident on her face.

"She used to write human-interest stories—fluff pieces—but I've seen a shift in the stories she'd been doing lately. More hard-core about different crimes. This caught my eye because the slant was like her old human-interest ones."

She would continue to run and hide, and she hoped stay ahead of any would-be killer. Schooling her features into a neutral expression, Hannah released a slow breath and swung her attention back to Caroline. "I'm glad they found that woman's killer."

"Me, too."

Hannah leaned back, relaxing as much as she could with all that had happened. "Has Austin called again?"

"He'll be home soon with Big Red. Our neighbor wasn't too happy to find him in his pasture. The man's stallion was hurt in a territorial fight. Big Red was hardly touched."

"At least now all the animals are accounted for, and Austin is pulling them closer in and posting more guards 24/7. I'm glad last night he posted a couple of men at the old barn or it might have been set on fire, too."

In the doorway into the living room, Barney lifted his head, then lumbered to his feet, his tail wagging. Austin came from the back of the house and stooped a moment to greet the dog and scratch him behind the ears.

The tired lines on his face stood out even more as Austin met Hannah's gaze. He pushed up and entered the room. "The sheriff will be here soon."

Caroline rose. "I'm going to leave you to talk to him. All this is catching up with me. I'm going to retire early like Misty." She stopped next to Austin and hugged him. "Gil will find who's doing this. I have the prayer team at church praying he's brought to justice soon."

"Thanks, Granny."

After Caroline left, Austin made his way to the couch and collapsed next to Hannah. "And thanks for picking Barney up."

"Misty and Caroline enjoyed getting away for a few hours. We even went to lunch at a café in town."

"When this is over, I'd like to take you out to dinner in Sweet Creek. There's a wonderful restaurant that serves a great steak." He rested his head on the back cushion, his half-veiled gaze fastened onto her face.

"You don't have to do that. What about Misty?"

"I think I can persuade Caroline to watch her for a few hours. You've had few breaks. This wasn't meant to be a 24/7 job."

"I like what I'm doing, and I did get away a couple of times. Remember the riding lessons."

"We can continue them again when there's less going on around here." His hand covered hers on the couch between them.

The physical contact accelerated her pulse rate. "What happens if the sheriff can't figure out who did this?"

"I'm learning not to worry about the future. To live for today."

"Not always easy to do."

He chuckled. "A year ago I wouldn't have been able to utter those words. But with all that's happened that's about all I can do. The future is in the Lord's hands."

"I wish I—"

The doorbell chiming cut her off. She rose. "I'll get it. You've been wrestling with Big Red."

The fact that Austin didn't protest spoke of how exhausted he must be. As she left the room, she glanced back at him. He closed his eyes, his chest rising and falling gently. His features relaxed into a calm façade.

When she answered the door, she allowed the sheriff into the foyer. "Austin's in the living room."

"I'm glad he found Big Red. That horse may be temperamental, but he's one fine stud."

Austin straightened when she and the sheriff entered the room. The calm expression vanished, and tension descended over his features. "I'm hoping you have good news."

"Nope. I wish I had the culprit in my jail, but I don't." The man sat on the edge of the chair across from the couch, his knees wide, his hat in his hand dangling between his legs.

"What about Bob Douglas? Where was he when the fire occurred?"

"According to his aunt who he was staying with, on his way to Colorado to get a new job. She says he left on Saturday, the day before the fire. She wasn't too happy with you by the way and had a few choice words concerning you. I haven't been able to confirm that's where Bob is."

"Kenny Adams?"

"His wife says he was at home asleep, as most people are at that time, she pointed out to me."

"Do you believe her?"

"Don't know. Mary protects her own so she could be lying." The sheriff played with the brim of his tan hat.

"Slim Miller?"

"Haven't been able to find him. No one has seen him in the past month."

"So no one has been ruled out." Austin sank back against the cushion.

"Nope. I want to rule out Bob first, so I've concentrated my investigation in that area. Can you think of anyone else who might have a grudge against you?"

"No, Gil. Most of my cowhands have been with me for years."

The sheriff shifted his attention to Hannah. "Can you think of anything else about yesterday morning? On the way to the barn did you see anything out of the ordinary? A truck or car you hadn't seen before? Or had and shouldn't be where it was?"

Hannah shut her eyes and tried to picture the walk to the barn. She'd marveled at the beauty of the hoar frost. Austin's SUV was parked in front of the house under the carport. A white pickup was next to the bunkhouse. She knew that one belonged to the foreman. She thought back over the other vehicles around the compound, and suddenly she remembered something.

Her eyes bolted open. "There was a black car with a smashed bumper. I saw it at the side of the barn away from the bunkhouse. Actually all I saw was the front of it, but I recalled the bumper on the left side was caved in."

The sheriff's gaze brightened. "I know who has a car like that." He stood, setting his hat on his head. "I'm gonna pay Mary and Kenny another visit this evening. I'll let you know what I find out."

Austin clambered to his feet. "Hopefully this will end it."

Hannah remained seated while Austin walked the sheriff to the door. Their murmurs drifted to her. Why hadn't she remembered that yesterday?

When Austin came back into the living room and took the place next to her, she shook her head. "I should have recalled that. It vaguely registered on my mind, but I was trying to keep up with Misty and enjoy the beauty of dawn. I'm sorry I didn't—"

Austin put his finger over her mouth to still her words. "There's nothing to be sorry about. I don't expect you to know every vehicle at the ranch, especially as I'm hiring new hands."

"I'm usually very aware of my surroundings, but the hoar frost was especially gorgeous. It was so heavy it almost appeared as though it had snowed and I love snow." *And I had been trying to figure out what was going on concerning the women killed in Montana by hit men—at least according to Violet.*

He trailed his finger from her mouth along her jawline, catching some hair and hooking it behind her ear. "I thought it was Bob for sure."

"So did I. Things don't always appear as they seem." Like the last day in Billings? Had she overreacted to the black SUV behind the taxi? Or her house being broken into? Should she have waited before fleeing the Witness Protection Program?

"But now that I think about it, Kenny was furious with me when I wouldn't hire him this year in January." Austin's brow furrowed.

"Why wouldn't you?"

"I'd caught him a couple of times drinking on the job toward the end last September. He's one of my seasonal workers, but the past few years he'd changed, become unreliable. I know he's been picked up for drinking and driving. I think his license has been suspended. When he came out here in mid-January about the job and I turned him down, he cussed me out then stormed away. That night he got drunk and ended up wrecking his car."

"The smashed bumper I saw?"

Austin nodded. "From the rumors I've heard from some of the men, Kenny's drinking has only gotten worse. But Gil will get to the bottom of it. If he presses Mary, she'll come clean about whether Kenny was there or not." He lifted some hair that fell over her shoulder and ran it through his fingers. "So what night do you want to go out to dinner?"

"Don't you think we need to make sure Kenny is the arsonist?"

"Give me something to look forward to. These past few months have been tough."

"Okay," she said with a laugh. "How about next Monday night? That should give the sheriff enough time and something for you to look forward to all week."

Austin moved closer, inches from her. "Oh, more than enough time."

The whispered words warmed her cheek and sent a tingle down her length. "We can celebrate two things. The next day I take Misty into Missoula to get her casts off and you get a day off."

"You don't want me to go with you?"

"No, I want you to spend the day carefree and enjoy yourself here at the ranch. You deserve it."

"But—" Again his finger silenced her words.

"I'll feel guilty if you don't. I don't want to be accused of overworking you."

"I don't think you are."

His finger traced her lips in a slow caress. "But I have an image of being a fair employer. I can't jeopardize that. You're just gonna have to take the day off. Granny and I will be back with Misty before dark."

He grazed his lips over her cheek, inching closer to her mouth. When he possessed it in a deep kiss, Hannah's world exploded in a burst of sensations, all centered on the man gathering her to him, his arms stroking the length of her back.

"So Kenny has fled the area?" Hannah leaned back against the deck railing along the front of the house, clasping it while facing Caroline.

"That's what Gil said when he called Austin a while ago. When he went to see him last night after talking to you and Austin, Kenny was gone for the evening. The sheriff went looking for Kenny at all his usual haunts in the county. He left a deputy at the house."

"And Kenny knocked the deputy out. He sounds like a man who is losing it fast."

"That's what I think. Gil was livid that Kenny had attacked one of his deputies then escaped. He'll be caught. He made a mistake going after one of Gil's people. He's got the word out. It's only a matter of time." Caroline picked up her knitting needles and yarn from the basket at her feet. "I feel so sorry for Mary. I think I'll take her a basket of food."

"Even after what her husband did to you all? For that matter she lied to the sheriff."

Caroline caught her gaze. "If the Lord can forgive us our sins, then I can forgive someone hers."

Hannah remembered the heat from the fire, the smoke-filled barn and didn't know if she could. The fact Misty still awoke in the night, in a cold sweat, sobbing, only confirmed that feeling. What would have happened if Misty hadn't made it out? Or all the animals died in the fire?

"You've got a few hours of free time. What are you going to do? It's a beautiful day. The first day of spring will be here soon. Actually the weather feels like it's already come." Caroline began to work on a navy-blue sweater for Austin.

"I think I'll go for a walk. Like you said, it's beautiful, not a cloud in the sky. Do you want to come?"

"My leg is giving me problems. You go without me today."

"Isn't Austin at the birthing shed?"

"Yeah, the cows are dropping their calves right and left, but that's a good thing. He likes to be in attendance or one of his cowhands to make sure everything proceeds correctly. No sense losing a calf, if it can be prevented."

"That's not that far. Isn't it down that road?" Hannah pointed to the right past the cleared area of the barn.

"Yes, about five hundred yards. Not far over that rise. Since most of the men are working on the barn or out watching the herd, he's left to do that."

Withdrawing the monitor from her jacket pocket, she put it on the brown wicker table next to Caroline. "I'll be back in an hour or so."

"Take your time. If Misty wakes up, I'll sit in her room and entertain her. She's been wanting to learn to knit. I was thinking of showing her a way using her fingers so when she gets the cast off next week she can exercise those fingers she hasn't used in a while."

Hannah descended the steps and started down the road, passing by the workers who were working on the barn frame. The sound of hammering echoed through the air. She could recall stories of people helping neighbors raise a barn in a day back in the past. The occasion would become a social gathering for the area. Did anyone do that anymore?

She knew Austin had gotten calls from his neighbors about helping him any way they could. He'd declined, knowing it was a busy time of year for them, too. He'd then gone to town and hired a few extra men to help with the barn.

The sun beat down on her, warming her, as she strolled toward the birthing shed, which if she remembered on her tour of the ranch was a small barnlike structure. At the top of the rise she scanned the area, drawing in deep breaths of the pine-scented air, fresh, crisp. The light breeze played with the long strands of her hair. A magpie, mostly white and black like a penguin, perched on a branch of a bare tree studying her. She smiled at it, relishing the peace and quiet in a crazy world. She could get used to living here.

And that was the problem.

She couldn't live here too much longer.

But she wouldn't think about that right now. She would enjoy the day and maybe spend some time with Austin.

That thought spurred her forward on the road that ended at the birthing shed. She heard voices coming from it. The door was ajar, and she moved toward it to check and see who was with Austin. She didn't want to disturb him if there was something wrong with one of his cows.

She peeked through the crack.

A thin man—taller than Austin—stood with a two-by-four in his hand, his stance rigid as though readying himself to attack Austin, who was backed into a corner of the shed. A cow with a newborn calf nursing turned her big brown eyes at the explosive scene.

"You've ruined my life." The intruder's words came out in a seething stream of hate.

"Kenny, I didn't—"

"Shut up." With a surprised quickness, Kenny took a swing with the piece of wood, the flat of it connecting with Austin's shoulder as he twisted away, deflecting it some with his motion.

But the suddenness of Austin's movement caused him to stumble. He went down.

EIGHT

Kenny brought the piece of wood down again on Austin, but he rolled to the side, the end catching him on his thigh. The pounding sound of the two-by-four connecting with dirt floor reverberated through Hannah's mind. The next blow could be fully on Austin. She had to do something—quick.

Without her cell on her, she had no way to call for help, and if she went for it, the fight could be over, leaving Austin injured possibly. She searched the ground for anything she could use.

She snatched up a rock as the sound of another thump of the wood shuddered down her length. A lowing noise from the cow followed, making a mockery of the situation taking place in a shed where new life came into the world. She wanted to sneak up on Kenny from behind, but when she eased the door farther open, it creaked.

Hovering over a downed Austin, Kenny glanced in her direction and straightened.

"Get away from him," she said in her toughest voice that ended in a squeak.

Kenny laughed and raised the wood to swing again. Hannah rushed forward, realizing she wouldn't make it in time to stop the hit. Frantic, she threw the rock at Kenny's back as hard as she could.

It clobbered him right under the shoulder blade. The thin man let out a howl of rage and spun toward her. She glanced at Austin trying to rise. He stumbled forward.

Kenny advanced toward her, rage in his bloodshot eyes.

Maybe she could outrun him.

His diamond-hard stare bored into her and trapped her gaze. Hannah took one step back. Then another. She could make it down to the barn where the rest of the men were.

"Get out! Now or I'll—" Kenny shook the two-by-four at her "—take care of you then finish with him."

His look reflected the fury and desperation that had pushed the man over the edge. It held her immobile, her mind void of any solutions.

She took another step away. With her back pressed against the wall next to the door, she spied a pitchfork out of the corner of her eye. If she could get hold of that before he covered the distance between them, then maybe—

Austin barreled into Kenny, sending them both forward and crashing to the ground. The impact dislodged the piece of wood from the man's grip. It flew toward her. She ducked to the side and it clamored against the wall. She grabbed it, trying to figure out how she could stop the fight.

She inched closer, the two-by-four clutched in both hands and pointing to the ceiling.

But before she could decide how to use it without hurting Austin, he struck his fist into the man's jaw. Once. Twice. Kenny's eyes rolled back then closed. The noise of the blows vied with the agitated moos of the cow at the back of the large shed. Austin clambered to his feet, groaning with movement.

He looked toward her, his gaze filled with pain. But a slow grin spread across his face. "You're a sight for sore eyes, but if you ever do something like that again, I'll…" His threat faded into the silence as he shook his head.

She launched herself into his arms, Austin wincing at the contact. "I'm sorry." She eased back a little. "Are you okay? Where do you hurt? He could have killed you. I had to do something fast. I…"

Austin quieted her with a hard kiss. "I mean it. Don't do something like that again. I can take care of myself."

She pulled back farther and glared at him. "I saved you. The least you could do is give me credit for it," she said in a mockingly stern voice.

His smile widened. "That you did. You gave me the time to recover enough to take care of him." Austin threw a glance toward Kenny.

The man moaned, opened his eyes but they quickly slid close again.

"I'll go get help now." Hannah turned toward the door.

"Good idea." Austin sank against a post and slipped down to the ground, groaning with each movement.

Several squad cars were parked in front of the building where Saul Peterson lived. Micah didn't like that. A bad feeling knotted his stomach. Saul Peterson was his only lead on Jen Davis/Hannah Williams.

Micah rode the elevator to the third floor and when he stepped off, his gaze immediately riveted to the older man's apartment number. A police officer stood outside.

Not a good sign.

He strode toward Peterson's place. The officer latched on to his approach and straightened away from the wall.

"Can I help you?" the Billings policeman asked.

Micah showed the man his U.S. Marshal ID. "I am here to talk with Saul Peterson."

"He was taken to the hospital half an hour ago."

"What happened?"

"Someone broke into the apartment and beat him up. The detective on the case is still inside. The crime tech guys haven't come yet. Do you want to talk to him?"

"Yes." Micah's gut constricted even more. A robbery gone bad? Or something connected to the Martino Chicago crime family and Jen Davis?

The officer opened the door and called the detective.

When the man appeared in the entrance, Micah stepped away from the uniformed officer. "May I have a word with you?" He again presented his identification. "What happened to Mr. Peterson?"

"What's your interest in him?"

"It's a case I'm working on, and I'm not at liberty to say anything."

"Was Mr. Peterson in your program?"

"No, but I'm following a lead. Did Mr. Peterson say anything before being transported to the hospital?"

"No, a cleaning lady found him and called the police. He was unconscious when she found him and didn't wake up by the time he was taken to St. Vincent. I'm finishing up here then going over to the hospital to see if he's regained consciousness yet. He was beaten pretty badly. Actually I'm surprised, considering his age, that he's alive."

"Were there any signs of robbery?"

"I don't think this was a robbery. The obvious items stolen are still in the apartment but it is apparent someone searched his place."

Micah withdrew his card. "If you discover any more

information concerning this break-in, please give me a call."

Micah quickly left and drove the short distance to St. Vincent Hospital. He found the emergency-room doctor who was treating Mr. Peterson. "What's his prognosis?"

"He's in critical condition. He's in a coma. We've treated what we can and now it's in God's hands."

"He never woke up?"

"No."

"If this changes, please call me and let me know."

Micah left the building and retrieved his cell from his pocket. A few minutes later his brother, Jackson, came on the line. "We've got a problem. I think a hit man has found out where Jen Davis is. I was following a good lead concerning her whereabouts. I think she worked for Saul Peterson up until a couple of weeks ago. Someone beat the man nearly to death. I think for information."

"Keep looking for her and let's pray Mr. Peterson wakes up and can give us some information before anyone from the Martino crime family discovers Jen Davis's whereabouts."

"I will. I'm going back over to his apartment and doing my own searching. Maybe there will be something there to indicate where she is."

Monday evening Hannah sat across from Austin at a table for two in a restaurant that specialized in serving the best steak in Montana. "I now see why people come even from Missoula to eat here. The meal was delicious."

"You deserve every bite of it. And more. Kenny is in jail. I'm healing, thankfully, but I'll remember that fight for a while."

"At least you aren't limping anymore and—" she

flashed him a grin "—trying not to wince every time you move."

"Isn't there a saying about time healing all wounds? In my case it has—mostly. So I'm glad we could still celebrate tonight. My barn is nearly finished. Misty gets her arm cast off tomorrow and maybe even the other one. Life is good."

Almost perfect. But Hannah wouldn't tell Austin about her woes. He couldn't do anything to change them, and she couldn't stay no matter how much she would love to. The Triple T Ranch and his family were his life. Hers was somewhere else.

"That poor cow with her calf." Hannah lifted her water glass and took a drink.

"She was glad to get out of the birthing shed, but I was glad I was there for the calf's birth. That one I had to assist with."

"Do you have to help usually?"

"No, but enough about the ranch." He grinned. "What are you gonna do tomorrow? If you want, you can borrow a vehicle and come into town or go anywhere you want. You aren't confined to the ranch."

"The ranch is fine with me. I thought I would explore the woods and small lake you have on your property."

"Just so you know, occasionally I get hunters and other tourists on my land. Usually they wander off the Rocking Horse Ranch where they come to hunt, hike or fish. I don't allow hunting or, for that matter, hiking on my property. I used to let the hikers go until a few caused some damage. I have to redirect the parties back to where they belong. Although there shouldn't be any hunters, wear something bright."

"I have a red jacket." Thankfully she was partial to the color since she didn't have a big wardrobe.

"That'll work. I want you to have fun tomorrow."

"It's supposed to be the last pretty day before a cold front and snow comes in. I'm going to be outside enjoying it and the ranch."

He cocked his head to the side. "You do enjoy the ranch, don't ya?"

"Yes, why wouldn't I? It's gorgeous. When I look at your ranch, it's so easy to see the Lord's hand in its creation. A masterpiece."

"I love hearing someone talk like I feel about my ranch. I think it's a little piece of paradise."

"I guess there are some who might not see it that way, but I feel like they must be blind."

His chuckles peppered the air like the aroma of grilling meat coming from the kitchen. "You're my kind of woman."

His words colored her cheeks with warmth. She averted her gaze from the sudden intensity flowing from him as though he'd reached across the table and wrapped his arms around her, nestling her against him.

"I'm sorry your wife didn't see the beauty in the Triple T," Hannah said in an attempt to put some distance between her and Austin. *Because in the end I'll be doing the same thing: leaving him.*

"So was I. Misty deserved more than that from her mother."

"You deserved more." *And I have to remember that.* But Hannah's heart twisted at the thought of leaving him in a month.

"Hey, I didn't bring you all the way into Sweet Creek for a night on the town to talk about my late wife. That's my past." He reached across the small table and clasped her hand on the white tablecloth. "I'm learning not to look back but forward."

And the expression in his eyes emphasized his developing feelings toward her. The admiration she saw constricted her throat. She swallowed several times but nothing cleared the jammed emotions.

She gently tugged her hand from his and rose. "I need to visit the ladies' room. Be back in a minute."

Quickly she weaved her way through the tables to the restroom. Inside she leaned into the marble counter and stared at herself in the mirror. She wore her only nice "fancy" dress from when she'd lived in California, a sleeveless, black sheath with a scooped neckline and silk fabric that draped in soft folds. She'd borrowed Caroline's black cashmere sweater since she didn't have anything that really worked for this type of restaurant. Her long, chestnut hair fell in waves about her shoulders. But the expression in her eyes—large pools of conflict—at the moment gave away how in over her head she was with Austin. She so wanted to grab what Austin was hinting at—a serious relationship that could possibly lead to something permanent.

She couldn't. Slamming her palm down on the counter, she wanted to scream in frustration. She was so out of her element—physically and emotionally. Tomorrow she had some serious thinking to do on her hike.

Before he came searching for her, she washed her hands then left the ladies' room. When Austin saw her making her way toward him, he rose, placing his linen napkin on the table. The smile that caused his face to glow with happiness pierced straight through her heart.

"I've taken care of the bill. Let's go. I thought we might walk along Main Street, do a little window-shopping. A few places remain open until nine on Monday night."

"We don't have to do that if you need to get back to the ranch."

He grasped her hand and strolled toward the front door. "I don't and I want to. You're right. This may be the last warm evening, and it's so nice out. Sometimes those cold fronts move in earlier than we expect."

"I'm hoping it holds off until at least dark tomorrow night. I have big plans to commune with nature. I'm going to take my camera and get some pictures."

Outside on the sidewalk on Main Street Austin started toward where most of the stores were located. "You like to take photos?"

"Love to. This state is perfect. The only downside is my camera doesn't do justice to the grand scale here."

"I'd love to see some of your work."

"I have a scrapbook." Not a large one since she moved all the time, but one that let her have a piece of something she loved to do.

"You constantly are surprising me. I wouldn't have taken you for a photographer."

"What does a photographer look like?"

"Someone with a camera hanging around their neck." Austin shrugged. "Honestly I have no earthly idea."

"Well, for your information I'm not a photographer. I take pictures. That's all."

He paused at a store window with sports equipment. "Okay, how about skiing? Do you do that?"

"Nope. I can't see myself flying down a mountain at breakneck speed—for fun. Do you?"

"I grew up here, so, yes, I do. I loved doing it especially when I was young."

"Versus being old?"

He laughed. "When I was younger."

At the next shop Hannah stopped and looked at the books on display. "I love to read, too. Can we go inside?"

"Sure. I've been known to read."

In the bookstore Hannah separated from Austin, exploring the different sections of categories. A good story allowed her to live a life she might never have since her options were limited. She glimpsed one she thought she might like in women's fiction, a multiple generational saga, set in Montana, and decided to buy it for the long nights when she was alone in an apartment in some other state. When she was gone from Sweet Creek, Montana, and the Taylors.

"Ah, there you are. Ready to leave? I think the lady is wanting to close up."

"Yes." Hannah went to the counter and paid for her book, then left with Austin.

Taking her hand again, he slowly strolled toward where he'd parked his SUV. The feel of his fingers around hers was so natural that the very thought scared Hannah. She should pull away. She didn't.

When they arrived at his red Jeep, Hannah sighed, hating that the night was coming to an end so soon. She'd forgotten what it was like to be on a date. This evening made her dream of what she couldn't have.

He settled his hands on her shoulders, stopping her from slipping into the front seat. "I enjoyed this evening a lot. We need to do it again soon."

"Yes," she murmured as his fingers kneaded the tightness in her muscles. "I'd like that." *Too much.*

His mouth hovered above hers, and she fought the impulse to rise onto her tiptoes to shorten the distance between their lips. Finally he brushed his mouth over hers, then took hers in a kiss that zinged her clear to those tiptoes. When he parted, the glimmer in his eyes, revealed by the streetlight nearby, heightened the spiraling sensations tumbling through her.

He quirked a grin. "We'd better get going before the town of Sweet Creek starts talking."

She clutched the SUV door to keep her legs from melting into a quivering pool on the pavement. Inhaling gulps of the cool air, she stared down the street as she tried to shore up her defenses. It was useless. They lay crumbled at her feet.

Shaking her head, she started to duck to get into the Jeep when her gaze caught sight of a big Ford-150 truck. Black like the night. Two men sat in the cab, and she was sure they peered directly at them. She felt their eyes on her. Shivering, she hurriedly slid onto the seat, not taking her gaze off the truck.

Not ten seconds later, the black vehicle roared to life and pulled away from the curb, heading in the opposite direction from the ranch. She blew out a long breath. Just her imagination again. Violet's suspicions were making her more paranoid than usual. But the fact she had to be constantly on the lookout for strangers only reinforced that anything started with Austin was doomed before it began.

"Are you sure you don't want me to come to Missoula with you?" Hannah asked above the sound of a buzz saw.

Austin slammed the car door. "Yes, I'm sure. I want you to enjoy my ranch. Take a pickup or a golf cart to the lake if you don't want to walk. The keys are on the pegboard by the back door."

She should argue with him, go with Misty to the doctor's, but she had some thinking to do and every time she was around Austin he disrupted her train of thought. This was better. Besides, they were a family and should spend time together without her around. She needed to stop integrating herself into their activities and put some physical and emotional distance between them and her.

As Austin rounded the back of the SUV, Hannah opened the door. "I have some fun things planned for us when you get back home." She grinned at Misty. "Just think, you'll get to throw both arms around Candy's neck tomorrow."

The little girl's eyes gleamed with excitement. "And soon I'll be able to walk again." She thumped her leg cast, then leaned close and kissed Hannah's cheek.

"Safe trip," she murmured around the lump in her throat, peering into Misty's, Caroline's and finally Austin's face.

As he drove off, his car disappearing over the first rise, Hannah wanted to run after the SUV and demand she go with them. She didn't need a day by herself. She'd have a lifetime for that.

Burying her face in her hands, she kneaded her fingertips into her forehead. She had it bad. In less than a month she'd fallen in love with a wonderful man and his family.

What am I going to do?

Noise from the hammers and other equipment being used to finish the barn intruded into her mind. She couldn't think here. The temperature was nearing fifty, and it was still before noon. Staring up at the sky, she noticed the azure blue stretched as far as she could see, disappearing behind the mountains in the distance.

She spun on her heel, marched up the steps to the deck and let herself into the house. She was going to do exactly what she said she was going to do and spend the day at the lake. Water was always calming. She could remember visiting the beach in California and listening to the waves crash against the shore. Rhythmic. Luring.

A lifetime ago. Sighing, she shoved those memories away.

Quickly she gathered some food for a picnic, putting it into her backpack, changed into her hiking boots and snagged her red jacket and digital camera. When she emerged from the back door, she ignored the vehicles Austin had offered her and headed across the field in the direction of the woods and lake. She needed to walk and think.

The sun warmed her in a matter of minutes. She slipped out of her jacket and tied it around her waist. The forecast for tomorrow was snow—lots of snow. She could hardly believe that would happen, but she'd lived here long enough to realize it was a definite possibility.

As she neared the woods that surrounded the lake, she spied a herd of elk trotting across the meadow and vanishing into the pine forest. She managed to snap a couple of photos. Eager to reach her destination and eat lunch, she entered the woods. Sunrays dappled the ground, forming a checkerboard of light and shadows. The area was surprisingly clear and easy to traverse through.

When she came into view of the lake through the stand of trees, she hurried her pace, nearly tripping over a fallen branch. Slowing her gait, she proceeded with more caution. She didn't need to hurt herself and not be able to get back to the house. When she reached the shoreline, she shrugged out of her backpack and sank onto a boulder jutting out over the water. All she wanted to do was drink in her surroundings—the snowcapped mountains, the lake, the tall pines that enclosed her in her own world. Peaceful.

Peaceful. The word taunted her.

After the incident at the end of the previous evening in

Sweet Creek with Austin, this morning before everyone was up, she'd sneaked into Austin's office to use his computer to do a search on the Internet. She should've waited until he'd left for Missoula or until she asked him if she could, but she hadn't slept at all the night before.

She'd panicked yet again with those two men sitting in the truck a block away. She realized she needed to know what had really happened two years before when she'd run away and dropped out of the Witness Protection Program because she thought someone sent by Devon had found her and broken into her house. She wasn't sure she could find the answers, especially if it had been one of Devon's men.

But after only twenty minutes, she'd discovered the truth. Her house had been one of many in a series of robberies that had plagued the small town until two teens had been stopped. She'd fled for no reason.

So did she want to contact the U.S. Marshal's office in Billings and let them know where she was?

As long as she followed their rules and never tried to contact her family in California, she would be all right. They could relocate her to a different state because when she left Austin she couldn't stay in Montana. Too many painful memories.

Then she remembered what Violet had said about a leak at the U.S. Marshal's office. She couldn't contact them. She would have to leave Montana on her own.

Before she walked away from Austin when his daughter didn't need her anymore, she would tell him everything. Although that conversation would be hard, he deserved to know the whole truth about her. But one thing she would keep to herself: that she loved him.

Her future decided, Hannah slid off the boulder and

strolled toward her backpack on the ground. Hungry, she sat and unwrapped her sandwich.

After lunch she snapped a few more pictures, then stretched out on the soft pine needles that covered the ground and used her backpack as a pillow. Staring up, she noticed a couple of white fluffy clouds sailing across the sky. Her eyes drooped closed and with the sounds of the birds chatting in the trees, she slipped into a dreamless sleep.

Austin felt like celebrating. The news from the doctor was good. Misty's bones were healing well, and he had gone ahead and put her in a leg immobilizer, instead of another cast. She still couldn't bear weight on her leg and would continue to use the wheelchair, but the doctor was happy with his daughter's progress.

Only a couple of miles to the ranch. He couldn't wait to tell Hannah. She would share his joy and that fact made him smile. Granny had a feeling about Hannah from the first. That she would be perfect for the job. She was and much more.

Thank You, Lord, for bringing Hannah into our lives—into mine.

Less than a half a mile from the turnoff for his ranch, he spotted a black truck off the road in a small clearing. The vehicle, a brand-new shiny one, didn't look familiar. He'd keep an eye out when he got home. Hunters sometimes wandered onto his property although he had signs up saying, "No hunting. No trespassing." He loved the fact elk and deer ran freely on his land. But some of his neighbors supplemented their income by hosting hunting parties and other tourists.

Ten minutes later he pulled up to the front of the house,

barely containing his eagerness to see Hannah. They'd only been gone six hours. Shorter than he thought. Probably because he'd wanted to get back to the ranch—to see Hannah.

"I'll get the wheelchair," his grandmother said as she climbed from the car.

"That's okay. I'll carry Misty to the deck." With adrenaline pumping through his system, he could easily take his daughter to her wheelchair.

After settling Misty, he opened the front door for her and his grandma. When he entered, he knew immediately Hannah was still out by the lake. The house felt empty, too quiet.

"Granny, can you take care of Misty for a while?" he asked as his daughter made her way toward her room.

His grandmother's bright eyes twinkled. "Going to find a certain young lady?"

"I saw a truck back not too far from our gate. I want to make sure no hunters are on the property."

"Sure. That's all you're going to do?" she asked with a laugh.

"Okay, I'm gonna head for the lake after I check on the progress at the barn because I want to see Hannah. There, I admitted it to you."

Grinning, his grandmother waved her hands. "Go. Have some fun. You certainly deserve it. Misty and I are going to practice her finger knitting now that she has the use of both hands."

He walked through the house, searching to make sure that Hannah was really gone and to tell his daughter he'd be gone for a couple of hours. Standing on the back stoop, he noticed the vehicles he'd told her to use if she wanted were still parked where they'd been that morning.

That gave him an idea. He'd saddle two horses. Hannah could ride back on her mare. Or if she didn't feel confidant in her new skills, she could ride double with him. Actually that thought appealed to him a lot.

But it would be Hannah's decision. He wouldn't push her into something she wasn't ready for. From the beginning he sensed she held something back. He wanted to know everything about her because he wasn't going to fight the deep attraction he had for her anymore.

A rustling noise, as if squirrels scampered across dry leaves, woke Hannah up. Her lower back ached from lying on the hard ground, but she didn't hurry to sit up. Instead, she took a moment to orient herself to her surroundings. The lake. The forest behind her, which would account for the sound. She stared straight up at the clouds thickening, turning darker.

And then she noticed the chill whispering across her front, the cold earth seeping through the thickness of her coat and jeans to make lying on the ground doubly uncomfortable. She rolled to her side and glanced at her watch. It was getting late and the clouds were moving in fast. The temperature felt as though it had dropped fifteen or twenty degrees since she'd arrived. Hannah rose and gathered up her belongings, then hiked toward the woods a hundred feet away.

Going what she thought was due east, she picked her way through the maze of predominantly tall pines. Their scent hung in the air, giving off a clean fresh aroma. Voices drifted to her, and she slowed her pace, trying to figure out where the sounds were coming from. There was a slight echo through the trees. She wanted to avoid meeting any people, but perhaps she first needed to figure out where those men were so she could evade them.

Tilting her head and listening to the male voices, she tried to catch what was being said. The murmurs quieted, but she thought they came from the right. She snuck closer and saw two men, dressed in jeans, flannel shirts, jackets and hiking boots. The thin guy carried a rifle. The other didn't. One hunter and the other coming along for the ride?

They stopped. Hannah hid behind a tree, flattening herself against its rough bark.

"I think we're going around in circles," the thinner of the two men said in a low voice she strained to hear.

"We need to pop our mark and get out of here before it gets dark."

Mark? Hannah tensed. *The hit men Violet had told her about?*

"This time we need to make sure it's Eloise Hill or the boss is gonna have our heads."

"This one fits the description. We saw that last night." The more muscular one pointed toward the way she'd come, not far from where she was hiding. "She's here somewhere. She went in and hasn't come out."

I'm not Eloise Hill, she wanted to shout, trying to pick up what else they said.

"Let's go that way. It doesn't look familiar."

"How can you tell?"

The thin intruder frowned. "I just can."

"Yeah, you're a regular Boy Scout." The muscle man cackled.

"Shh, we're getting close to the lake. We can't mess it up this time."

Mess it up this time? Those two murders Violet told her

about? Those women's deaths really were murder by hit men? Confusion mingled with Hannah's mounting fear.

Please, Lord, let this all be a mistake. No hit men. No women murdered. No one who has mistaken me for this Eloise Hill.

As they got closer to the water, she saw her chance to make a break for it. If they kept going, they would be at the lakeshore, and she could get away without them knowing. Heartbeat thundering in her ears, she darted from one tree to the other, trying to hide as much as possible.

She peeked around the large trunk. The muscular man separated from the thin one, making his way deeper into the forest instead of toward the lake. She had to get help.

Backing away, she pulled out her cell to call 911. When she stepped on a limb, it snapped in two, the sound reverberating through the trees. She looked down, then jerked her head up. The heavier-built intruder pivoted, and fifty yards away, his gaze fastened onto her.

She whirled around and started running as fast as she could, her hand still gripping her cell but not daring to take the time to make a call. Help wouldn't come in time. She had to do something. Now.

Zigzagging through the woods, her back tense in anticipation of being hit with a bullet, she frantically searched the terrain for an escape, a place to hide. Anything.

Lord, I need help!

The thrashing sound of the big man behind her spurred her faster. Pain seared her lungs. Her legs burned. Her side felt like a knife kept stabbing it.

Suddenly she plunged forward, her body impacting with the hard ground. Her cell flew from her grasp.

NINE

Austin guided his gelding into the woods on a familiar trail that led to the lake nestled at the base of a mountain. There was a chance he and Hannah would miss each other if she went a different way. He constantly scanned the terrain to keep an eye out for her red jacket. He couldn't wait to see her. Hold her. Kiss her. He'd missed her today while in Missoula.

A sound to his right alerted him to movement. Hannah? An elk? Something else? A large man was running. He stopped and lifted his hand—holding a gun. Not a rifle.

Austin turned his horse toward the intruder and peered at the area he was aiming. Something was on the ground. A wounded animal? Hannah!

The air rushed from Hannah's lungs from the collision with the forest floor. Cell? Where was it? Panic spiked her heartbeat rate. A sharp stone cut into her palm.

Through the pounding in her head, she heard the pounding of approaching steps. No time to look for her cell. Run!

She shoved to her feet, starting forward before she'd fully straightened. Slightly in front of her something struck the tree trunk and wood sprayed outward. A piece sliced across her cheek. Without thinking she lunged behind the pine.

Can't outrun a bullet.

Help, Lord!

Austin pulled his rifle from the scabbard, lifted it and sighted the assailant stalking Hannah. With a calmness he hadn't thought possible, he squeezed off the shot. Then another—both meant to wound, not kill. The man went down, the gun flying from his hand.

Urging his horse forward, he rushed toward the fallen target, sweeping the area for anyone else. "Hannah, stay where you are."

Still clutching the rifle, Austin leaped from his gelding and hovered over the man, his weapon pointed at the attacker. Blood oozed from his left shoulder and the fleshy part of his thigh. Pain carved into his features, he groaned while feeling around him for his lost gun with his good hand.

"Who are you?" Austin seethed, his gut churning.

The man fixed his hard gaze on Austin, giving up his search for his Glock. But he didn't say a word.

"Hannah, are you all right?" Austin shouted, deciding the sheriff could sort this all out.

"Yeah."

Her voice came from behind him only a few feet away from him. "What part of stay where you are is unclear?"

"Austin, I've got his gun. There's another man with this one." Hannah stood behind Austin. "He has a rifle. We need to get out of here."

"You won't get away, Eloise," the man on the ground uttered, a laugh escaping him.

Its sound chilled Austin. *Who's Eloise? Hannah?*

What's going on? Question after question demanded answers but there was no time.

Austin positioned his body between Hannah and her assailant. "Untie the mare's reins from my saddle and get on her." As Hannah grasped the reins, Austin backed away from the shooter, his rifle still pointed at the man's chest.

"I can't ride her." Her voice shook as her body did.

He wanted so badly to hold her, calm her fears, but instead he said, "Grip the reins. Hold on to anything but stay on her."

His rifle cradled against him but still aimed at Hannah's attacker, Austin lunged toward her, patting his thigh. "Use this to get on her."

She started to hike up her leg when a crack frightened the mare. The horse pranced, backing away, eyes wide. Hannah immediately let go of the reins she still held.

Austin dove toward Hannah at the same time another rifle shot thundered through the forest. He rolled them down an incline that would partially protect them from the new threat coming from the direction of the lake.

He fumbled for his cell in his jean pocket and handed it to Hannah. "Call 911."

As she reported what was happening, he kept a vigilance on the woods, trying to see where the man was holed up. Depending on how good a shot he was, he could be hundreds of yards away. He zeroed in on his cohort trying to crawl away, his blood staining the earth.

"You might tell your partner the sheriff is on his way."

"You'll be dead before he arrives." The large man spoke in a hoarse whisper as he gave up moving and sank to the ground, moaning.

"I'm not this Eloise Hill you're looking for." Then louder Hannah repeated that sentence as though she hoped that would stop the other assailant.

He needed to find where the man was located. Austin stuck his head up a few inches farther and a bullet whizzed by, nicking his scalp.

"Let my foreman know what's happening. We need help. Tell him the man is just in the forest by Crescent Point." Austin gave her the number.

"You're bleeding." Her voice quavered.

"It's nothing. At least now I know where he is. Max can get here in fifteen minutes. He was an Army Ranger. He'll know what to do." Because the man was right. They could be dead before the sheriff arrived.

The sight of Austin's blood flowing from his head threatened Hannah's composure more than the man had chasing her. She'd never wanted this. And the thing was these men here had nothing to do with Devon Madison. Eloise Hill? Who was she? What was going on? She'd never had the time to search the Internet for Eloise Hill. Why hadn't she done that first? Because after not discovering much on the two women's murders, she hadn't thought there was anything to Violet's theory.

"Max said he'd call when he took care of the man by the lake." The assurance in his foreman's voice didn't calm her. She quaked so badly she finally thrust the gun she'd picked up from the ground at Austin. "I'm afraid I'd shoot myself. I don't like guns."

He laid it in front of him on the ground, using a tree and the ditch to protect himself enough to keep watch on any movement. "Just stay down no matter what happens while we play this waiting game. Do you know who this Eloise Hill is?"

"I don't know who she is."

The minutes ticked excruciatingly slow. She tried to inhale deep breaths to calm her rapid heartbeat, but all she did was gulp in shallow ones. Watching the second hand go around and around on her watch only frazzled her nerves even more. She tore her gaze from it.

Then a thought intruded. What if the goon with the rifle made a wide circle to come up behind them? Flipping onto her back, she searched the woods behind them, not sure what she would do if she saw him creep closer. But at least she knew what he was wearing and could possibly see something.

The ring of Austin's cell jolted her. She flipped it open, her hands trembling so much she almost dropped it. "Yes?"

"This is Max. Tell Austin the man was here, but he's gone now. We found some spent cartridges at the scene. His footprints are heading away from the woods along the shoreline. Several of us are tracking them. A few more are making their way toward you, combing the area as they go."

"Thanks." Hannah ended the call and peered toward Austin. "The man's gone. At least that's what Max thinks. They're checking it out while others are coming this way."

"I see Rodney." Austin cautiously stood, shielding part of himself with the tree and shouted, "We're over here."

Five men, all carrying guns, converged on them. Hannah stayed on the ground in the ditch as two of the hired hands hauled the assailant up while one retrieved Austin's gelding about a hundred feet away. They slung the would-be killer over the saddle, none too gently.

Hannah turned away and kept her gaze trained on the forest behind them. Just in case, she told herself, but really she didn't want to look at Austin at the moment, not with blood matting his hair, trickling down his neck. It only emphasized what could have happened earlier if the bullet had been an inch to the right.

"Hannah, are you ready to go?" Austin said slightly behind her and to the side. "One of the men found the mare. We can ride together back to the ranch. I found your cell."

She clasped her knees to her chest. No matter how much she hugged herself she couldn't stop the fear tumbling through her. Her whole body shook so badly she didn't think she could stand. She could have lost Austin today. Misty could have been without a father and mother. She couldn't get that out of her mind.

"Hannah? Are you okay?" Austin knelt in front of her.

Her gaze riveted to the bullet graze on the side of his head, the red mocking her with the type of life she had been forced to live. She couldn't take her eyes off the sight.

He grasped her upper arm and, with his finger on her jaw, swiveled her attention toward his face. He smiled. "The cavalry arrived in time. We're safe. We can go home now."

The soothing cadence of his voice tempted her with the idea she was truly safe. But she knew the truth. She would never be safe, and now she knew he would never be safe with her near. That one day in her life five years ago had changed it forever. If only she hadn't been…

"Hannah, you're worrying me. Talk to me."

His fervent tone drew her back to the here and now. She blinked, focusing on his endearing face, the smile that warmed her cold, cold body. "I'm okay," she said slowly, trying desperately to believe those two words.

"Let's go home. The temperature is dropping fast."

"Yes, home," she whispered, wishing she had one.

Austin shrugged out of his overcoat and slipped it around her shoulders. "I'm gonna help you up and onto the horse. Okay?"

She nodded.

His arms about her made her want so much more in her life. His support as they walked toward the mare, cocooned for the time being in a shelter of protectiveness she knew wouldn't last long. She leaned into him, drawing on the solace of his strength.

He mounted the mare, then reached a hand down to her while Rodney formed a step by interlocking his fingers together.

"Boss, we'll take this one back for you." Rodney tossed his head toward the assailant strapped to the gelding's saddle. "Max called to say that they tracked the footprints back to a place along the highway where it looks like a pickup was parked."

"I think it was a black, Ford-150 truck, new, clean. I saw it earlier."

Like the one in town last night. She hadn't overreacted for once.

"I'll call that in to the sheriff so they can be on the lookout for one," Rodney said as he walked toward the gelding.

Austin gripped the reins. The muscles in his arms that touched her bunched. "I'd like to get my hands on that guy."

"If he's smart, he's long gone." Rodney led Austin's gelding away.

Austin directed the mare toward the edge of the forest, near where she'd come into it hours before. An eternity. He didn't say a word on the long ride back to the main house. But he held the reins in one hand and clasped her to him with his other arm. Exhausted, she laid her head back against the cushion of his shoulder. His warm breath fanned her neck. The gentle rocking of the gait lulled her into a trance she welcomed.

The sight of the house, the sheriff's car parked next to it, aroused Hannah from her daze. She didn't look forward to being involved with a law enforcement agency yet again in the area. She didn't want some inquisitive sheriff delving deeper into her life. She had caused havoc not once but twice in a short amount of time in his county.

Thank You, Lord, for Your help. I would have died back there if it wasn't for You. Austin would have, too. Now I have another request. Help me make it through the interview that is surely going to follow. The fact she was so automatically praying again was a marvel to her and gave her some peace.

Dusk cloaked the landscape as Austin dismounted and held his arms out to help her down. She practically fell into his embrace. He gave a hired hand the reins of his mare, and then without a word, led her up the steps to the deck. Caroline threw open the front door, her mouth etched in a frown, worry in her eyes.

"Gil told me what happened," Austin's grandmother said, placing a hand on her arm. "Come in. I've got a fire going. You two must be cold."

"Is the sheriff in the living room?" Austin entered his house holding Hannah against him as if he were afraid to let her go.

Caroline nodded. "I'll get something for you two to drink and keep Misty away."

"Does she know anything?" Austin asked.

"No. I made sure of that. You might go see her when things calm down." His grandmother shifted her attention from Austin to Hannah. "You, too. She's been wondering where you are. She wants to show you her arm and what she has on her leg now."

Hannah wanted to postpone the interview with the

sheriff for as long as possible. Maybe then she could have made some sense out of what happened and have something to tell the man. "Let me go talk to her for a minute." Hannah slipped from Austin's embrace and almost crumpled to the floor if she hadn't clutched the table nearby.

Austin wound his arm around her again. "We'll go together."

She didn't argue with him, but when they drew close to the child's bedroom, she halted. "If I go in with you supporting me, she's going to know something happened. And one look at your wounded head will alert her something is wrong."

He stepped back, holding her at arm's length. "I'd say we both better do something about how we look."

"Listen, I can make it." She straightened her shoulders, pressed her lips together and lifted her chin a notch. "I'll change and go see her. You talk with the sheriff. I'll be in there by the time you finish. Then you can clean up and see Misty."

"Are you sure?"

"Very." Because she had to be. She didn't want to alarm Misty, and she needed time to compose herself before talking to the sheriff. And at the moment Austin's nearness complicated things.

As he saw her to her own bedroom door, she stiffened her resolve. She'd lived with fear for five years. This was really no different. Falling apart didn't accomplish anything. By the time he left her, she knew what she needed to do. Slowly she undressed, her movements jerky. After she donned another pair of jeans and a sweatshirt, she examined herself in the mirror in the bathroom and saw the haunting linger of terror in her eyes.

Somehow she had to camouflage that from a perceptive little girl. Concentrating on the positive—she and Austin were alive—she washed her hands and face, cleansing the cut on her palm and cheek with some peroxide. She could keep her hand hidden, but she would have to come up with something to explain the scrape on her face.

At the entrance into Misty's room she heaved a breath, forced a smile to her lips, hoping it reached into her eyes, and thrust open the child's door.

"Hannah, look at my arm!" Misty held it up, waving it. "And this." She pointed toward her leg immobilizer.

"That looks great to me." She crossed the bedroom to the wheelchair and kissed the girl on the top of her head. "It won't be long before this will come off, too." Gesturing toward the immobilizer that encompassed her whole leg, she gave Misty a hug, wishing she could hold her the rest of the night.

But the sheriff waited.

"What happened to your face?"

Hannah touched her cheek. "I wasn't looking where I was going and fell in the forest."

"Daddy said you went to the lake. Did you see any animals?"

"Yes, some elk, ducks, geese. And I heard an owl but couldn't find him."

"When I get my cast off, can we go to the lake for a picnic?"

"That sounds nice," Hannah said because she wouldn't promise something she didn't know she could do.

Caroline came into the room. "Hey, I'm ready for a game of Go Fish. How about it, Misty?"

"Sure, Granny. I can hold the cards better now."

"I've got to leave you for a while, but I'll be back later." Hannah hugged the child one more time, then left while Caroline settled into a chair nearby to play Go Fish.

When Hannah entered the living room, Gil and Austin stopped talking. She lowered herself down next to Austin on the couch. His hand immediately covered hers on the cushion between them.

"Austin was just telling me about what happened when he found you. I'd like you to tell me what happened, especially before Austin appeared." Gil held a pen, and a pad sat on his thigh.

"I fell asleep at the lake. When I woke up, I noticed it was getting late so I decided to head back to the house."

"So what happened next?"

"I headed into the woods. Not too far in, I heard some men talking in low voices. I thought they might be lost like the other one, so I went to check them out." She slanted a glance at Austin, whose expression grew tense. "Or hunters who were hunting something illegally."

"Were you planning on saying anything to them?"

Hannah tried to think back to the time before everything exploded and she had to run for her life. "I don't know."

"Austin said the one he shot talked about an Eloise."

"Yes, they mentioned looking for an Eloise Hill. One of the men had a rifle and the other a handgun. I thought that was strange even if they were trespassing."

"Did you hear what they were talking about?"

"Some. They talked about getting their mark and this Eloise Hill."

After scribbling something on the paper, Gil asked, "You don't know anyone by that name?"

"No. You don't know anyone in the county called Eloise Hill?"

"No, and Austin said he didn't, either."

"So who is Eloise Hill?" Austin tightened his hold on her hand.

"That's a good question because it looks like someone wants her dead."

She leaned toward the sheriff. "You've got to warn this woman." She remembered her own terror in the woods and never wanted another to go through that.

"I'll be asking around. Make sure she isn't here on vacation. I'll put something out to other law enforcement agencies in the state. Maybe they had the wrong location."

"A case of mistaken identity?" Austin leaned back on the couch, pulling Hannah close as though he would protect.

"That would be my guess. You said the guy said Hannah looked like this Eloise Hill."

"Who is the guy?" As Austin slung his arm around her shoulder, cradling her against him, she relaxed some of the tension building in her.

"Harry Milton from Chicago. He clammed up and asked for a lawyer. I couldn't even get the name of the guy with him or where he had been staying while here."

"Chicago? That's a long way from Montana." Austin drew slow circles on her upper arm.

"That's what I'm thinking. I'm gonna do a little checking up on this dude while he's getting patched up at the hospital. I know someone with the Chicago police. I'll call him and see what he can run down for me." Gil rolled the pen between his forefinger and thumb.

"Hannah, anything else you can think of?"

"They took one look at me and pursued me so I must really look like this Eloise Hill. I'd be dead if Austin hadn't shot the man. He'd already shot at me once."

"If either one of you think of anything else, please call." The sheriff rose and put his pad in his shirt pocket. "I'll keep you informed about what's going on." He peered right at Austin. "I'm posting two deputies outside. I don't think either one of you are in danger because I'm sure Harry's partner is long gone, but I like to cover all my bases."

Austin shook Gil's hand. "Thanks. Anything you can do is appreciated."

A memory flashed into her mind. "Wait, Sheriff. I have thought of something else. They also mentioned something about messing up before and not wanting to make their boss angry."

"So they could have killed or attempted to kill before. I'll check about unsolved murders recently and see what I can find out." He tipped his hat toward Hannah. "You've been a big help."

While Austin walked the sheriff to the front door, Hannah paced. Maybe the sheriff could find out if those two women were murdered and if it appeared as though the killings were a professional hit. If she could, she would flee the ranch and Montana right now, but she couldn't with two deputies guarding them and a hit man still on the loose. So the next best thing was discovering all she could about Eloise.

When Austin reentered the living room, he took one look at her and asked, "What have you thought of?"

"I want to do an Internet search for an Eloise Hill. What do you think?"

"That's a great idea. Let's go into my office and see what we can come up with."

"It'll probably take a while."

"You can start the search while I shower and pop in to

talk to Misty, then let Granny know what's going on. We'll take a break for dinner, but even if it takes all night, I want to track down all references to an Eloise Hill on the Net."

Well past midnight Hannah finally found something on Austin's computer that interested her. "Take a look at this," she said when he came back into his office with two mugs of hot chocolate.

He hovered behind her right shoulder, placing her drink on the coaster next to the computer. "This reference is about an Eloise Hill in Chicago who testified against Salvatore 'No Conscience' Martino twenty-two years ago in a murder and extortion trial. After the trial she disappeared."

Hannah pointed at the screen. "The mafia kingpin is still alive. It doesn't look like for long, though. It says the old don served five years and got out on a technicality. Some people wondered what happened to Eloise." Clasping her mug in her cold hands, Hannah twisted around to look up at Austin. "Did Salvatore's thugs get rid of her? Or are they searching for her in Montana?"

TEN

"This could be the Eloise Hill they're looking for." Austin settled his hand on her shoulder. "Or not."

"This is the best possibility so far. They're from Chicago and so was this Eloise woman, but I know Chicago is a big town." She turned back to the screen and printed the information concerning Eloise Hill who had gone missing years before.

"There is another thought. What if she went into the Witness Protection Program?"

Hannah tensed, her eyes squeezing closed. The words he uttered struck too close for comfort. Why was there a hit out on this Eloise Hill after twenty-two years? What had changed? Was she still in the Witness Protection Program? Were the U.S. Marshals protecting her somewhere or did she flee their protection like Hannah had? And what about the possible leak? The questions triggered fear. "It's definitely a possibility."

"First thing tomorrow morning I'll call Gil. He can give the U.S. Marshal's office a call about what happened. Who knows? If she's in federal protection, his call will alert them that someone is looking for her. It might save a life."

"That's what's important." She wanted to tell Austin not to call Gil because there could be a leak in the U.S. Marshal's office, but what reason could she give? Maybe, though, if the sheriff stressed that Hannah wasn't Eloise Hill, whoever leaked the information would let the Martino crime family know she wasn't the woman they were searching for.

She brought her mug to her lips and took several sips, hoping her quavering hands weren't visible to Austin. Those thugs hadn't been after her, but that could have been her as the target if Devon Madison ever found her.

Austin reached around her and picked up the sheets she'd run off. "You know, this old picture sure does look like you."

Hannah laughed shakily. "Yeah, but she's probably ten or twelve years older than me. I don't think I'm flattered that those thugs mistook me for a woman who has to be forty at the very least."

"What makes me wonder is how those men ever picked up on you in the first place?"

She wanted this conversation to come to an end. It was moving into uncomfortable territory with questions she had no answers to. She wished she did, but she didn't want Austin or the sheriff delving too much into her background. There was no long-term background for Hannah Williams.

Hannah rose, cradling her mug between her hands. "Did one of your employees say something about a truck parked off the highway near your property? They tracked the other shooter back to some tire tracks."

"That's right. I think that was the black Ford-150 I saw on the way home from Misty's doctor."

"Last night in Sweet Creek I saw the same kind of truck

parked a block away from where your car was. There were two men in it. I was sure they were staring at us, but then they drove off." She started for the kitchen. "Do you think they spotted me in town and thought they had found the Eloise Hill they were hunting?"

"I guess they could have. But why Sweet Creek? I know we aren't too far from Missoula and it could have all been a coincidence, but still..." He left unsaid all the doubts she had about the whole situation.

In the hallway she angled toward Austin. "We may never know the whole story. Harry isn't talking, and if he works for the mob, I doubt he will. By now his lawyer has probably arrived."

"Then we need to make sure the sheriff gets it across to Harry and his lawyer that you aren't this Eloise Hill."

"That might not convince them."

"You're at least ten years younger. If they got an up-close look at you, they would see their error. And one thing about our good sheriff. He's mighty convincing." Austin plucked the mug from her hands. "You go to bed. I'll put these up in the kitchen. We may know more tomorrow. And don't forget we have two deputies guarding the house and a manhunt out for the other shooter."

She stifled a yawn. "My day off didn't quite turn out as relaxing as I thought it was gonna be." Traversing the length of the hall to her bedroom, she leaned against her doorjamb. "Next time you offer me a day off, I think I'll stick to working. Besides, being with Misty and helping her and Caroline isn't what I consider work." She bent toward Austin, getting a good whiff of his masculine scent. "But don't tell my boss that. He might expect me to work for free."

"Oh, I don't think you need to worry about that. I hear he's a pushover for a beautiful woman."

The heat of a blush stained her cheeks.

He brushed a finger over those cheeks. "I think you could even persuade him to allow you to sleep in tomorrow. You certainly deserve it."

The mind-shattering sensations assailing her from all angles at his mere touch nearly overwhelmed her. She clutched the doorjamb tighter. "I'll take that under advisement. I'm so tired, but I don't know if I can sleep much. I'm afraid every time I shut my eyes I'll relive that man chasing me through the woods."

He tweaked her nose and stepped away. "If that's the case, I'll know where to find you. In the kitchen warming some milk. I may be joining you. It isn't every day I shoot a man."

She studied the almost neutral expression on his face—except she glimpsed the regret and remorse in his eyes. She wouldn't expect anything less from Austin. He wouldn't be a man who could take a life easily, even when it was justified. "You didn't have much of a choice, and this woman is very happy you did. I'm just glad you had a rifle with you."

"I always do when I go too far from the main house. Every once in a while I've encountered a bear on my property. Sometimes wolves or a mountain lion. A shot in the air will scare them off and that will be the end of it. The lake area has always been safe, but it's a habit to take my gun more now than a necessity."

"I hope they find that man's partner. I'd feel better if they do."

"So will I. I gave Gil a pretty good description of the truck I saw parked off the road not too far from the

Triple T turnoff. He sent that information out immediately. Maybe something will come of that."

Tears threatened when she thought again of what could have happened today if Austin hadn't come to her rescue or if he'd been killed trying to help her. She didn't understand the thugs coming after her even with the information she read about Eloise Hill. She didn't even know if that woman was the same one they had been after.

She did realize she could never put Austin in danger and needed to leave sooner rather than later. She had some thinking to do in the next day or so. It wouldn't be easy for her to leave with no means of transportation and an ongoing investigation being conducted with her at the center.

"Good night, Austin. I'm so sorry this happened today."

As she turned to go into her bedroom, he stopped her, moving close, his hands clasping her upper arms. "Why are you apologizing? You had no control over what went down today. If I hadn't come in time, do you realize what I would have felt like, finding you shot on my property?"

Through a blurry mist, she took in the anguish in his expression. A pressure in her chest expanded outward. No, she didn't have anything to do with what was going on with Eloise Hill, but she had been in the Witness Protection Program, probably the same as the woman the thugs were after today. The earlier incident made her realize she needed to leave, not put people she loved in danger. She could and had lived with the constant fear, but she couldn't live with herself if something happened to Austin, Misty or Caroline.

"Hannah, please tell me you aren't blaming yourself for what happened." Austin framed her face with his large, work-toughened hands, his thumbs smoothing away the tears leaking from her eyes.

"I wish I could. But I do."

"You have no control of what those men thought. I can see from a distance you look like this Eloise, but up close they would have seen you're too young. I think the one I shot had figured that out when he finally got a good look at you, but the other was at least a hundred yards or more away."

"And he's still out there. I should leave here." *I'm used to running and hiding. The only thing different is that it will be two I will be running from.*

"And do what? Go where?"

"You don't need to worry about that."

Anger flared into his eyes. "I don't!" His voice lowered, a hard edge to it. "What kind of man do you think I am that I would let you go off by yourself and try to deal with this on your own?"

"One who is alive. That's what!"

"Do you not realize I'm in this as deep as you are? I was just as involved as you were out there in the woods. There are two deputies in this house. I know the ranch and I can defend it. If you were somewhere new, you might not know what is normal, who to trust. Here you do. You can trust me."

His fury blasted her in her face. She blinked the last of her tears from her eyes and lifted her chin. "What about Misty?"

"I'm taking her and Granny to my sister's in Missoula tomorrow. They'll stay there for a few days. By then we'll know what we're dealing with. My grandmother and, for that matter, Misty would never forgive me if I turned you out to fend for yourself."

Hannah sank back against the doorjamb, so tired her brain felt like mush. "I don't know what to think anymore.

I…" She couldn't even finish the thought, all words flying from her mind.

"Are we clear about what we're going to do for the next few days?"

She nodded. For the time being she would see what the sheriff could do and what he heard back from the U.S. Marshal's office.

Lord, as today, it's in Your hands.

"Good, because I've come to care about you a lot and don't want anything to happen to you. Just remember you had nothing to do with causing this. We'll get through this together."

Tell him.

She would have to soon when she wasn't so wiped out. She trusted him with her life; she would trust him with the truth about who she really was.

He drew her to him and encircled her in his embrace. "You saved my daughter's life in the barn. Let me protect you. I owe you."

She pressed herself against him, wishing she never had to let him go. But there would come a time when she would. Soon.

Light leaked into Hannah's bedroom from the slit in the curtains. She groaned and rolled over, seeing the time. Eight-thirty and yet she felt like she'd wrestled with a grizzly all night long.

Throwing the covers back, she dragged herself from the bed and padded to the window, pushing the drapes back to allow more light into the room. A snowy white landscape greeted her. The storm had finally arrived, and big flakes fell as she looked out onto the pristine scene. In the distance she glimpsed the new barn. It had been

Austin's priority to have it finished before the snow came that the forecasters had been predicting all week, so he could stable as many of the horses as possible.

Quickly she dressed, feeling guilty that she'd slept in a couple of extra hours even if Austin had told her to. If Misty and Caroline were going to Missoula, she wanted to ride with them and say goodbye because there was a good chance she wouldn't be here when they returned.

She found the family in the kitchen, all sitting at the table finishing up breakfast. "Good morning." Hannah poured herself a big mug of black coffee and hoped the caffeine would sweep the cobwebs from her mind.

"You're up. Daddy is taking us to Missoula to see Aunt Kim. We're gonna stay a few days." Misty drank the last of her milk.

"You sound pretty excited." Hannah sat in the empty chair across from Austin.

"I have two cousins I can play with. Of course, they're boys." She arranged her features into a look of tolerance.

Hannah chuckled. "How old are they?"

"One is four and the other is eight." Austin lifted his drink and took a sip. "I talked with my sister, and she was happy to have a couple of visitors. Granny and you will have fun." He directed his last statement to his daughter.

"Hannah isn't coming, too?" Misty asked, popping into her mouth the last of her strawberry jam covered toast.

"Not enough room at Aunt Kim's." Austin finished the last of his scrambled eggs.

"She can share a bed with me."

"That'll make it a bit crowded. You and I are sharing a guest bedroom and there's only twin beds." Caroline stood and took her empty plate, utensils and glass to the sink. "I'm going to pack my bag then yours. Want to come help, Misty?"

Misty maneuvered her wheelchair toward the door, stopped at the entrance and glanced back. "You are gonna ride with us to Aunt Kim's?"

"I wouldn't miss the trip," Hannah said around the lump lodged in her throat. She was going to miss the child.

Misty beamed. "Great!"

When the child left, Hannah looked at Austin. "Will Kim be okay taking care of Misty?"

"Yes. She's looking forward to it. You can show her what you do and the exercises the doctor sent home for Misty to do with her arm."

"Does she know what happened here?"

"Yes." Austin scraped back his chair and stood. "More coffee?"

"In a bit. What about the weather?"

"We'll be ahead of the worst of the storm. What fell last night wasn't much. As soon as Granny has packed we'll leave, and on the way back from Missoula Gil wants us to stop by the station. They have a lead on the second man, and hopefully he'll be in custody by then. You need to ID him. I didn't get a good look at him like you did."

"That's great. If they get him, Misty might not be gone long at all."

"That'll depend partially on the storm. The reports I've heard this morning aren't good. By night it is supposed to increase a lot. They're even talking about blizzard conditions."

Hannah glanced out the window at the light snow still falling. "I'll go help Misty with her things. We should get on the road."

* * *

"I hated saying goodbye to Misty." Hours later, Hannah stared out the SUV's windshield at the snow continuing to fall. She was glad she wasn't driving, and that Austin seemed so capable and not frazzled by it.

He slid a glance toward her. "It's not goodbye for long."

Yes, it was. The thought only made her want to cry. "I'm glad Gil called a few minutes ago to let us know they've picked up the other man." She shifted to stare out the back at the deputy's car following them. "I imagine they'll be eager to get home, too."

"I didn't want to tell you, but Gil said he wants to keep them with us for a while longer. He said he'd explain when I got to the station." Austin sent her a reassuring smile. "He didn't want me to lose focus on driving."

"That doesn't sound good."

"Me losing focus?"

"No, that he would be worried about it because of what he has to tell us." *What has the sheriff discovered?*

"We don't have much longer. We're almost there."

Chewing on her lower lip, Hannah turned and watched the snow blowing as it came down. The wind was really picking up.

Twenty minutes later, he pulled into the almost empty parking lot next to the sheriff's office. "We can't stay long. This is getting worse quickly, and it'll be dark in an hour. I don't want to be on the road when that happens."

"You won't get an argument from me." After buttoning her overcoat and putting on her gloves, she pushed open her door and walked into the wind toward the building, ice pellets stinging her face.

Her boots sank six inches into the snow on the parking lot. Freezing tentacles blasted her. She squinted against the onslaught and tried to see where the entrance was. Austin came up beside her, took her elbow and guided her toward the main door into the station.

"It's a good thing I've been here several times," he said as they entered with the two deputies right behind them. "It's hard to see with the wind and snow coming right at your face."

"I've got a feeling this storm is gonna be a bad one."

Gil emerged from an office behind the counter. "I'm glad you got back safely from Missoula. The timing for all this couldn't be worse. I wouldn't have asked you to stop if it wasn't on your way to the ranch. I'm changing out the deputies to give them a break with two new ones." He stepped out of his office doorway and gestured with a wave of his arm. "Come in here for a moment before you look at the second man."

Hannah's heart thumped against her chest, its beat increasing as she passed the sheriff and went inside.

Gil shut the door. "I called, as you know, Austin, first thing this morning the U.S. Marshal's office in Billings. I had to leave a message on a machine. All I asked was for someone to call me concerning an Eloise Hill. Finally an agent called me back an hour ago. I told him about the attempted murder and the two men I had in custody. I explained about how the assailants had indicated they were after this Eloise Hill and they thought you, Hannah, were that woman."

"But I'm not."

"The agent was quite interested in the incident when I said they had targeted Eloise Hill. Then I quickly told him that you weren't that woman. I described you to him and he agreed. He told me some things were going on here that he wasn't at liberty to tell me, but that he would put a message on the desk of the man in charge. He was leaving, but the other agent, a Micah McGraw, was due back in the office."

"But you haven't heard anything." Good, the sheriff reinforced to the U.S. Marshal's office she wasn't Eloise Hill. Just in case there was a leak there.

"Billings is getting hit, too. I don't think anyone will be going anywhere, but I'm a cautious person. I'm sending two deputies with you to the ranch to be on the safe side. The second guy was on his own for twenty-four hours. I don't know who he called or what he arranged. I told the marshal I would guard you and Austin until I hear from them."

"What if you don't hear from them?" Hannah grasped Austin's hand.

"That's not the impression I got from the marshal. I got the feeling the feds are interested in the two assailants I have in my jail. I'll hear something. It just might not be until the weather gets better."

"Let's go see this second guy. We need to get home." Austin moved toward the door.

The assailant with the rifle sat in the interview room, drumming his fingers against the table. Hannah stood at the two-way mirror and waited for the thin man to turn his head toward her. When he did, his ice-cold eyes bored right through the glass and into her heart. His pockmarked face would remain branded in her mind for a long time.

"That's him."

"Are you sure?" the sheriff asked to the left of her.

"Yes, I'm sure."

Austin draped his arm along her shoulders and cradled her against him. "Can we go now?"

"Yes. If I have any more questions, I'll call."

After a labored trek to the SUV, Austin turned the ignition on and let the car run for a couple of minutes before slowly pulling onto the road that led toward his ranch.

"Are you all right?" Austin's attention remained glued to the windshield.

"I'd feel a lot better if this was all over with. But at least both shooters are in jail." Noting the swirling snow, like a blowing white sheet enclosing the SUV, she added, "And no one in their right mind would be out in this kind of weather."

"Are you saying I'm nuts?" His laugh took the edge of chill off her.

"I guess we both are. We're both here." Hannah patted the leather seat.

"I've been living and driving in Montana all my life. We'll be okay. We just need to take it slow and easy."

"At least Caroline and Misty are safe and warm."

For a few seconds he shared a glance with her. "You really care about them."

"Yes. You've been blessed with a wonderful family." *I had one once. Now I'm as good as dead to them.*

"I know. I thank God every day for them."

"Yesterday in the woods the Lord answered my prayers. You came and then later we were rescued by your men."

"You sound like it was a surprise that He answered your prayers."

"I just never thought I was important enough for Him to care what happened to me. I'm a tiny fish in a big ocean."

"And now?"

"Maybe He does."

"I can tell you one hundred percent He cares and knows *everything* about you."

"If He answered my prayers before, I wished I'd understood what His answers were." So much heartache and tears could have been avoided.

"Maybe you didn't want the answer He gave you. It's hard for us to understand we don't always know what's best for us."

She so wanted to shout at Austin: *But I've suffered for five years. That isn't any kind of answer.* She clamped her teeth together and held the words inside. As she thought about them, she began to see that, yes, her life had been hard, but she hadn't really suffered. She had her health. She'd met some interesting people, like Saul Peterson, in her constant moving. She'd helped some in her job.

All those thoughts only added fuel to the confusion she felt over the past few days being mistaken for an Eloise Hill, probably a woman who had been in the Witness Protection Program at least for a while if not still now. The irony of hers and Eloise's lives didn't escape Hannah.

The blanket of white outside the window blurred as the exhaustion from the past couple of days finally crashed down on her. Her eyes drifted closed….

"Hannah, we're home. Wake up."

She heard the words through a long tunnel. She didn't want to wake up. But then the cold glass pressed against her cheek and the pain in her neck dragged her from the depths of sleep. She blinked her eyes open and peered outside the car. All she saw was white.

Unable to make out even the outline of the house, she angled toward Austin. "Are you sure? Where is it?"

He gestured toward the windshield. "I parked as close to the back door as possible. You stay where you are. I'll come around and we'll go together."

"Are the deputies here?"

"Yes, they made it. We drove, especially the last part, almost bumper to bumper."

Again she scanned the area around the SUV and really couldn't see much. "I'll take your word for it. Nothing makes a person feel more isolated than a blizzard."

"Nope. And you know not to leave the house once we get inside. You can get turned around in a blizzard and end up lost."

"I am now, but you didn't have to worry about me going out in this. What about the animals?"

"The horses have been brought into the two barns. The pregnant cows, too. The rest will have to fend for themselves. As soon as we can, we'll check on them and get feed to them. It's buckle-down time for everyone and everything."

"What if we lose power?"

"I have generators. You can quit worrying. I've been through this before. It might not last too long." He reached out and brushed his gloved finger along her jawline. "Okay, ready?"

"Yeah."

Austin opened the door and slipped out, but not before a blast of frigid air and driving horizontal snow invaded the warmth of the SUV. Hannah shivered and buttoned her heavy overcoat. By the time he held the door for her to exit the vehicle, she reminded herself how much she loved cold weather. But a few minutes later she was happy to be inside a toasty, welcoming home where the roar of the storm was muted some.

The two deputies stomped into the kitchen behind Austin and shrugged out of their coats. "Sir, I'm Brady and this is Tom." He pointed toward his partner, who nodded. "We're gonna check the house first, then one of us will be on guard while the other gets some rest. Then we'll switch. There will be one of us up and about at all times." With a glance toward the window, he grinned. "But truthfully I can't see anyone going out in this. So sit back and relax."

When the two men left the kitchen, Austin faced Hannah and took her hands, tugging her close. "Do you like to play Scrabble?"

"Scrabble?"

"I figure we have time to kill." His mouth tilted upward. "Excuse the use of that word."

With his warm expression drawing her, she snuggled closer. "I could say I like to go in for the kill when I play games. I'm very competitive."

"Ah, that sounds like a challenge—" he bent his head toward hers "—and I love a good challenge. This will be interesting."

The feel of his mint-flavored breath fanning her lips, the mischievous gleam dancing in his eyes all worked to undermine her resolve to try to put some kind of distance between them. As much as she wanted to surrender totally to him, she wouldn't, couldn't. And in that moment she knew she would tell him about her past—this evening. He might never know it, but it would be her one act of love—to tell him her secret that she hadn't told a soul in five years.

Hannah put the seven tiles on the Scrabble board. "I won!"

"I challenge that word." Austin sat back in the chair at the kitchen table and crossed his arms.

"*Favella* is a perfectly good word and gives me eighty-two points. That's what kind it is."

"Give me that dictionary." He waved his hand at the book lying next to her on the other side. "Aha! It's not in here."

"What do you mean it isn't? Let me see."

He slid the dictionary to her. "I see *favela* but not the other word."

"It's a cluster of spores. I promise. Go look at the dictionary online."

He huffed. "I trust you. Not every word is in that dictionary or I probably couldn't lift it." But a playful look glinted in his eyes. "Just remember that when I come up with a weird word because I definitely want a rematch."

She heard him talking but really didn't register much past the word *trust.* Would he trust her when she told him she wasn't really Hannah Williams but Jen Davis?

"Listen, Austin, I have something I need to tell you," she said as he studied the board.

He yanked his head up and held her gaze. "This sounds serious. Should we go somewhere more comfortable?"

"No, this is fine." She was afraid if she postponed it much longer she could chicken out. She was handing her life over to him essentially. Then she thought of the deputy in the living room who walked through here a couple of times an hour. "Well, maybe in your office where we could shut the door and have some privacy."

"If my interest hadn't been piqued before, it is now."

Hannah started putting the game back into its box. Another delay tactic, she realized. Her hands quavered, and she dropped a fist full of tiles.

"You okay?"

"It's been a long two days."

"Then why don't you wait to tell me until tomorrow and get a good night's sleep?"

Because now that I've decided, I won't get any sleep until I tell you. But it won't be easy. She put the top on the Scrabble box. "No, let's talk now."

Confusion and a hint of wariness darkened his eyes. Rising, he took her hand and drew her toward his office at the back of the house. She entered first, with him closing the door after he did.

He strode to his black leather couch and folded his long length onto it. "Okay, we're here and we have some privacy. What is it you want to tell me?"

She sat on the sofa at the other end, but restlessness sped through her. She surged to her feet and began to pace. "I'm not sure where to begin."

"Hannah, you're scaring me. What's going on?" Although he said the words in a calm, controlled voice, his mouth was pinched into a frown, his body taut.

ELEVEN

In the middle of Austin's office, Hannah whirled around and faced him, clenching her hands at her sides. "First, I want you to know why I'm telling you this now. I trust you. I care about you, Misty and Caroline."

Totally alert, Austin straightened. "What's wrong?"

"When I lived in Los Angeles, I witnessed a murder by the man I was dating."

"Is that why you left?"

"Yes. That incident changed everything. I'm not who you think I am. My real name is Jen Davis, but I haven't gone by that in five years. I have used various different ones over those years. My latest one is Hannah Williams."

His expression went blank. "Why?"

The word spoken with such control hit her like a huge wave when she used to surf. She wasn't doing this right, but then this wasn't something she'd ever done. The U.S. Marshal who had been her contact had always stressed how important it was to keep her identity hidden from everyone and especially from anyone in her family or Los Angeles. He hadn't equipped her with how to break the rule.

Pacing from one end of the office to the other, she tried

to bring order to her thoughts that had been swept away with the crash of the wave.

"Is this where you tell me you're running from the law?" His question punctured the long silence.

And she couldn't blame him for it. She halted and pivoted toward him. "I'm not doing this right. No, I'm not running from the law in L.A., but I am—avoiding the U.S. Marshals." She sucked in an oxygen-rich breath and looked right into those eyes that so often held a smile, a warmth. Neither was evident now. "I testified at Cullen Madison's trial, and he went to prison for murder. His brother, Devon, is a very rich and powerful man who didn't take kindly to that fact. I was whisked into the Witness Protection Program and placed in Montana."

"Why are you avoiding them?"

"Two years ago there was a break-in at my house in a small rural community on the border with North Dakota. I thought one of Devon's henchmen had found me and panicked. I fled, leaving that life behind and have been on the run ever since. I didn't contact the U.S. Marshal's office when I was supposed to. I dropped off their radar."

"Did he find you?"

"No, since then I discovered my house had been one of several break-ins in that town over a period of a month. Mine being the first one."

He averted his gaze, a twitch in his jaw underscoring the tight restraint he was maintaining over his emotions. "Are you in the program now?"

"No, but I've decided after this is all over with, I'm going to contact them again and ask to be relocated to another area of the country. I've stayed in Montana long enough."

He reestablished eye contact. "So Hannah Williams will disappear? Or should I say Jen Davis?"

Her legs trembled so much she was afraid she couldn't remain standing. She sank into the hardback chair near his desk. "Jen Davis died five years ago. That woman had a caring mother and a younger brother who she loved and hasn't been able to contact in that time. When I walked away from L.A., I walked away from *everything*." Her voice cracked on that last word, remembering what that meant to her.

Something in his eyes melted, warming the brown depths. "You haven't contacted them once? Spoken to them? Wrote them?"

"No, the marshal I dealt with emphasized a clean break was the best. I'd be less likely to try to call them if I invested myself totally in my new life and the opportunities to start fresh." Her eyes misted; her throat contracted. "Maybe some can do that. I'm not one of them. You don't know how many times I've started to call my mom and hung up." A tear left a wet track on her cheek. She swiped it away. Crying didn't do any good. It didn't change her circumstances.

He stared down at his hands balled on the leather couch. "So what has been happening between us isn't real?"

I love you. That's about as real as it gets. "I won't deny that I have feelings for you and Misty. I do care, but nothing can come of it."

His head jerked up, and he stabbed her with a hard look. "Then why did you…" He snapped his mouth closed. "Never mind. It's not important." He bolted to his feet.

She rose. "Yes, it is. You want to know why I allowed these feelings we have for each other to develop when I knew it would end when I had to leave."

"Yes," he bit out between clamped teeth.

"Because I couldn't help myself. I—" *Fell in love with you and couldn't stop it.*

"What? That you like to toy with a man? How many men have you left when you pick up and move on to the next job?"

The force of his anger caused her to step back, hitting the chair behind her. Its crashing noise reverberated through the room. "None."

He laughed, no humor in the sound. "Oh, good. I'm the only unfortunate one to fall in love with you."

He loves me—or rather did. She wanted so badly to cherish the words, not uttered to her in years, but the look on his face spoke of the opposite now.

She drew up as tall as she could and squared her shoulders. "I don't toy with people's emotions. And I certainly didn't start out thinking that was what I was going to do as though that was my entertainment while stuck at this ranch." Her own fury welled in her at his rage that he had a right to feel.

"Stuck!" He closed the space between them, thrusting his face into hers. "You're exactly like my dead wife. So all the times you talked about loving the ranch and enjoying your time here were all lies like your name."

He'd taken what she'd said the wrong way. "I didn't mean that I was using you to amuse myself while here. I never felt stuck here."

Austin started to say something, but a knock at the door interrupted. He strode to it and opened it. "Yes?"

"Is everything all right in here? I heard something that sounded like a crash," Tom, the taller of the two deputies, said.

"I accidentally backed into the chair, and it toppled." Hannah bent and picked up the piece of furniture.

"Oh, okay. I was just checking to make sure everything was all right. You can't be too careful."

"Thank you, Deputy." Austin waited a moment while the man left, gripping the knob so tightly his knuckles stood out. "I think it's best you leave my office."

As she passed him, her steps leadened, he added, "I appreciate knowing now where things stand between us rather than the day you walk out."

"I'll leave as soon as the weather permits," she murmured, realizing that even though the conversation hadn't gone the way she'd planned this was for the best. Even knowing the contempt he felt for her right now, she was glad she'd told him. "Good night, Austin." The click of his door closing behind her echoed down the hallway as she trudged toward her bedroom.

Austin leaned into the door, his forehead against the wood. *Why, Lord? Why did You make me fall in love with her when You knew she wasn't staying?*

He shoved away and spun around, facing his couch. Seeing Hannah standing before him all over again, her words ripping a fissure through his heart. He never did anything impulsively, and he certainly didn't open himself up to others quickly. So why Hannah in less than a month? He'd have asked her to marry him rather than have her leave in a few weeks. Because the one thing he realized lately was that he wanted her in his life.

But she'd destroyed that dream.

He found his way to his desk, not even sure how he had, but suddenly he was in his chair, rotating it around to stare out the large floor-to-ceiling window. The snow had stopped since they had come into the room. Before him stretched a layer of white, in some places a foot and a half deep. Although after midnight, the landscape glowed in an eerie light for this time of day, almost as though the sun was rising hours early.

He needed to see to his animals, clear paths to the barn and bunkhouse… He needed to talk to Hannah, try to make some sense out of this hurt. He needed to— No!

Even if they talked and his anger and pain abated, she was right. There was no future for them. Ever. Bringing his fists down on the arms of his chair, he thrust himself to his feet and stood in the window, gazing out at his world. His life was his family and his ranch. A ranch that had been in his family for over a hundred and fifty years. He wouldn't leave here to hide like a fugitive in some faraway place as though he'd done something wrong. Not even in order to be with Hannah. He couldn't do that to Misty or Caroline. He couldn't do that to Hannah because he would grow to hate that life and then what kind of partner would he be for her?

He scrubbed his hands down his face, even surprised he was thinking about marriage, Hannah and what life would be like with her on the run, never feeling totally safe. The pain that ate into his gut should be enough for him to realize she'd betrayed his trust. She was no better than Jillian.

A few hours before dawn with the curtains open and the Bible Caroline had lent her in her lap, Hannah sat near her bedroom window watching the mantle of snow brighten the surroundings. The force of the blizzard had finally petered out, but in her heart the maelstrom of emotions assailing her hadn't. All night long, after leaving Austin in his office, she'd been battered and tossed about by those emotions until she now felt so lost as if she'd been out in the middle of the whiteout and couldn't find her way back.

Shoving to her feet, she paced from one end to the other. She had to make Austin understand she hadn't intended to hurt him. She hadn't intended to fall in love with him. That she bled as much as he did. But she didn't know how she was going to do that. The words still evaded her.

Lord, I can't do this without You. I know that now. Please give me the right words to say to Austin. I messed it up last night.

God is our refuge and strength. That verse from Psalm 41 seeped into her thoughts. *The words will come. He will be with me when I need Him.*

She pivoted toward the door and stared at it for a long moment. She couldn't talk to him now, but she needed to try in a few hours. When she turned toward her bed, its softness lured her forward. Exhaustion clung to every part of her. If she was going to make sense when she did talk to Austin, she needed some rest. She lay down on the coverlet and closed her eyes.

Austin stood before the mirror in his bathroom off his bedroom, the skylight illuminating the area as he stared at the dark shadows under his eyes. He needed to shave, get dressed in something other than his clothes from yesterday and go check on the animals now that the storm had passed and it was dawn. Gripping the edge of the counter, he leaned into it, so weary he really just wanted to go back to bed.

But then, why? He hadn't slept at all the night before. He couldn't get Hannah's confession out of his mind. Anger, like water just before it boiled, festered beneath the surface.

The quiet of his house taunted him. He hung his head and tried to drag to the foreground his determination to move on.

I can do this. She'll leave. I'll keep doing what I've been doing. Nothing wrong—

A creaking sound from a floorboard disrupted his pep talk. Hannah in his bedroom? His bathroom door ajar, he stepped to it and peered out, not sure he wanted to see her when his gut wrenched with the thought.

For a few seconds, he didn't see anything, then out of the corner of his eye, a bulky man came into his view. Not one of the deputies. Someone he'd never seen. Another thug after Hannah?

Every protective instinct in him vibrated to life. Stiffening, poised to surprise the man when he drew near, Austin waited, steadying his breathing to a calm level. His gaze riveted to the gun with a silencer on it. Its sight jolted him with the lethal implications.

He had to get to Hannah.

His nerves jiggled with tension. Each second that passed stretched his patience to the limit. His imagination ran rampant with thoughts of what could be happening to Hannah. But to leap now would be deadly to him.

The thug came another step closer to his bathroom.

The intruder opened his large walk-in closet door and went into it. Seeing his chance, Austin eased out of the bathroom and planted himself next to the closet a couple of feet away. When the man emerged, slowly, cautiously moving forward, Austin sprang from behind the closet door, bringing his arm down on the hand that held the weapon. But instead of the gun flying from his grasp, the man's grip tightened about his Glock.

The attacker swung toward Austin, only a foot away,

and charged into him. Austin held his ground, his back plastered up against the wall between the closet and bathroom. The gun between them, he fought to knock it from the thug's hand. The man's fierce expression filled Austin's vision as he desperately drew on a well of strength. His fingers about the Glock, too, he tried to direct it toward the intruder, but the man squeezed off a shot.

Pain ripped through Austin's shoulder.

Hannah struggled to breathe. A heaviness pressed down on her chest. Her eyes bolted open.

Devon Madison leered down on her as he straddled her on her bed. "Ah, you're awake. I don't want to kill you without you knowing exactly why you're going to die today."

His menacingly soft, cultured voice penetrated the sleepy fog about her thoughts. Her lungs burned. She tried to take a decent breath but couldn't.

He eased up slightly. "Sorry about that. I don't want you suffocating. I have other plans for you—much more painful." He ran his gun barrel down her cheek. "Have you heard my brother died in prison last month? Killed in a fight with another prisoner."

The air that flooded her lungs did nothing to relieve the tightness about her chest from panic. Although she heard his words, she tried to process what he was saying, but his handsome face with such a chilling smile riveted her full attention.

"So when I found out where you were, I just knew I had to do this myself. Sending someone after you wouldn't be as satisfying. I want to see the fear and pain in your eyes when I kill you slowly. You'll suffer, my dear. Just like my brother did behind bars for the past five years."

His seething hate exploded in her face, sending shafts of ice clear to her bones.

With her hands pinned to her sides and his weight keeping her constrained against the bed, she felt trapped like a deer surrounded by hungry wolves. She slid her eyelids half closed, refusing to let him see her expression as she frantically tried to school it into an expression that didn't show all the panic and terror consuming her.

He shoved the end of the barrel against her mouth. "Open your eyes or I might ditch my plans and feed you a bullet right now."

The pain, like a hot poker piercing Austin's shoulder, threatened to devour his strength and concentration.

Help, Lord.

Through the haze clouding his brain, Austin managed to focus on his attacker and throw his weight into him. Austin kept his hand locked about the gun as they tumbled to the floor, the bulky man taking the brunt of the fall. The impact stole the intruder's breath for a few seconds. Austin and the man wrestled for control of the gun. Suddenly the weapon discharged.

The thud sounded at the same time the bullet ripped through the assailant's stomach. He went slack, his clasp on the Glock dropping away.

Austin struggled to his feet, the scent of cordite swirling around him. The man's blood on his shirt mingled with his own, its metallic stench overpowering. From the hole in the man's belly, he wasn't going anywhere.

Austin staggered toward his dresser and yanked open

a drawer. Pulling a T-shirt from it, he held it to his shoulder and started for the door. No time to properly tend to his wound. He had to find Hannah.

Please, Lord, protect her. Keep her safe.

Out in the hallway upstairs, he scanned up and down it. How many men were in his house? Where were the deputies? As he headed toward the stairs, he stopped at the bedroom where the deputy slept and pushed against the slightly open door. The law enforcement officer lay on the bed, a gash in the side of his head, but the rise and fall of his chest indicated he was still alive.

The urge to go to him was strong, but Austin turned away, taking his cell out and making a call to 911 then to his foreman in the bunkhouse as he continued heading down the stairs. Austin kept his voice to a whisper as he talked, knowing help would probably be too late.

He hurried his steps, the increased movement making him light-headed. He steeled himself. He couldn't give in until he knew Hannah was safe.

As he crossed the foyer, he peered into the living room where the other deputy usually was camped out. At the entrance the man lay sprawled on the hardwood floor, a bullet hole in his chest. As though he sensed someone was near, his eyes fluttered open.

Austin knelt next to the deputy. "How many?"

"Two," the man choked out, swallowed then tried to say something else but went limp, his head rolling to the side.

Austin pushed to his feet, clutched the doorjamb to steady himself, then trudged forward toward Hannah's bedroom. As he drew closer, a male voice alerted him to the fact she wasn't alone. The other killer had found her.

Fortifying his resolve to end this now, Austin gripped his attacker's Glock and trained his full attention on her open door. Stealthily he moved toward the room and pressed himself against the wall.

The pain throbbing in his shoulder leaked into his thoughts as he listened to the killer say, "Good. You know how to follow directions. How did you think you would deprive me of seeing your fear? I've come all the way from California to see it."

Cold laughter filled the air, hardening Austin's heart. He'd have one chance to take this man out. With adrenaline pumping through him, Austin blocked the pain from his mind again and inched closer, peeping into the room to see where Hannah and the man were.

"You know I often wondered what my brother saw in you. Maybe I should find out before I kill you."

As Austin was about to make his move, rage blinded him for a few seconds. His hand holding the Glock shook. He froze in mid-motion.

Lord, help.

Suddenly calmness descended. Even Hannah's cry didn't pull him from his mission. Austin pivoted into the doorway, took aim and said, "Let her go."

The second intruder twisted about, leveling his gun up at Austin as the man pulled back on the trigger. Austin dodged to the side and got off a shot at the same time as Hannah's attacker did. A bullet struck the doorjamb a few inches from Austin's left arm, sending wood chips flying, while the man collapsed against Hannah.

The room spun before Austin's eyes. He sank to the floor, blackness hovering.

TWELVE

In the hospital's break room in Missoula, Hannah sat across from Deputy U.S. Marshal Micah McGraw from Billings. She interlaced her fingers together in her lap, trying to warm her cold hands that still slightly shook from everything that happened a few hours ago. But nothing helped. A chill had embedded itself in her bones the first time she'd heard Devon's cultured voice at the ranch, and it wasn't going to let go. At least not until Austin was all right.

"And you're positive the two men in the woods used the name Eloise Hill?" the U.S. Marshal asked, his dark eyes intent on her face.

"They mentioned that name several times. Is it the Eloise Hill from Chicago who testified against the mob twenty-two years ago that they were after?"

"I'm not at liberty to go into details, but you won't have to worry about those men anymore." Micah wrote something down in his pad. "Did the men from Chicago say how they found you?"

"No. All they wanted to do was kill me." A shudder ripped down her length, and she pulled the front of her sweater to her as she crossed her arms.

"Are you aware that Saul Peterson was attacked?"

Hannah sat forward. "What happened? How is he?" *Please, don't let there be another person I'm responsible for being hurt.*

"Monday someone beat him up in his apartment. It didn't appear to be a robbery, and Saul doesn't remember much about the assault. He's out of the woods and recovering at St. Vincent Hospital. I talked with him yesterday afternoon before the storm got bad. He'll be fine and is going home in a few days, Ms. Davis."

The use of her birth name took her by surprise. "So where do I stand with the U.S. Marshals?"

"With Devon Madison's death there is no threat to your life. And as he told you, his brother, Cullen, died in a prison fight a month ago. The thug with Devon told us that someone in the Martino mob sold the information on your whereabouts to Devon, but he's the only one who wanted it."

"Will Devon's man make it?"

"The doctor thinks so although he remains in critical condition."

"There's been too much death," she murmured. *A lifetime of it,* Hannah thought, her mind on autopilot.

Only Devon died out of all that carnage at the ranch, but the injury count was high—four. Three of them had been flown to the bigger hospital in Missoula. The deputy in the living room lost a lot of blood but would make a full recovery. The other suffered a concussion from Devon's bodyguard knocking him out as the deputy slept. And Austin was in surgery to repair his shoulder. She checked her watch. The minutes crawled by and still no report from the doctor.

"I don't often get to tell a person in the Witness Protection Program they get to resume their old life, but you do, Ms. Davis." Smiling, Micah rose and extended his hand. "Congratulations. I can arrange for you to fly to Los Angeles if you so chose."

Pushing to her feet, her legs wobbly, Hannah clutched the table's edge with one hand and with the other shook his. "I've dreamed of seeing my mother and brother again, but I've got to see Saul before I leave for L.A." Guilt weighed her down.

"You're free to see them, call them, whatever you want."

Whatever I want. I want Austin, but after all that had happened, that path is gone. One of the hardest things she'd had to do was call Caroline and tell her about Austin being shot and that he was in the hospital in Missoula. At least she and Misty could come and see him easily. She hadn't had a chance to talk to her when she'd arrived right before Micah McGraw requested to interview her.

"I'd better get back to the waiting room."

"I appreciate you talking to me at a time like this. I want to wrap this up and head back to Billings." He took out a card. "Call me if you need any assistance."

She slipped it into her jeans pocket, trying to smile but the effort was too much. "I don't know what I'm going to do yet. For so long I've been restricted in what I can do that…" She didn't have the words to explain the confusion and numbness she was experiencing.

"It's like you've been let out of prison?"

"Yes."

"It's sad that innocent people who try to help end up giving up so much because they do the right thing and testify. A few weeks ago I was sure I had found you in Billings until you gave me the slip."

"At the Carter Building?"

"Yes." Deputy U.S. Marshal McGraw opened the door for her.

"That was you. So I was being followed. I'd started to think I was being so paranoid."

"Apparently you have good instincts."

"Not good enough." She left the break room and faced him in the corridor. "People have been hurt because of me." And now she had to add Saul to the list.

"It wasn't you who brought those men to the ranch."

"How did they find me? I was very careful."

"I'm not sure. But we'll be looking into it. I'm hoping I can get more from the bodyguard and the two men sitting in Sweet Creek's jail. Good day, Ms. Davis." Micah nodded, then strode down the hallway toward the elevator.

She didn't know if she could go back to being that woman, Jen Davis. So much had changed in five years. She'd left Los Angeles so angry with the Lord for what happened to her. Now she saw He was the only way for her to come out of this sane. She had to lean on Him.

She made her way to the waiting room where Caroline sat with Gil, who had picked her up at her granddaughter's house. Hannah hesitated in the entrance, not sure if the older woman would want her sitting next to her, but she needed to explain, to ask her forgiveness.

Caroline spied her and rose. Using her cane, she made her way to Hannah, taking her into her embrace. "My dear, I've been so worried about you."

Hannah leaned back, not sure she heard Austin's grandmother right. "Worried about me?"

"Yes, Gil has told me what happened at the ranch."

"He did?"

"Austin is out of surgery and in recovery right now. The

doctor said he'll be fine. And both deputies will make a full recovery. Praise the Lord."

"But it's because of me that this all happened. I didn't mean for any of this to occur. I thought I was safe." Had she been deluding herself into thinking she was safe because of her growing feelings concerning Austin? She hadn't experienced something like that for so long—actually never, and for a few weeks she'd wanted to cling to that emotion of being cherished as a woman.

Caroline cupped Hannah's face. "I understand Devon Madison threatened you, hiring people to come after you. But it's over now. He's dead. You can't control what others do. Only what you do. You saved Misty's life a few weeks ago. You have been a breath of fresh air at the ranch. I haven't seen Austin so happy in a long time. Let's go wait in the room he'll be in. He should be out of recovery soon."

But Austin wanted nothing to do with her, especially now. How could he? He could have died because of her. Tears pooled in Hannah's eyes. "I'll be in there in a while. I have something to do first." She whirled around and hurried from the waiting room in search of the chapel.

When she found it, she collapsed into a chair at the front, finally releasing the tears she held back since the confrontation at the ranch early that morning. Now ten hours later her life was supposed to return to the way it was five years ago. But suddenly that wasn't so appealing.

Lord, what do I do? I feel so lost.

Outside the hospital in his car, Micah McGraw called his brother, the FBI agent in charge of the task force discovering the leak in the U.S. Marshal's office in Montana.

"Jackson, I just finished interviewing Jen Davis. At least she's alive and safe. I let Violet Kramer know about Jen and what happened at the ranch today with Devon Madison. I want her to do a story so there is no doubt in the Chicago mob's mind that Eloise Hill isn't Jen Davis."

"I heard from my informant. They've gotten that message, but it wouldn't hurt to reinforce it. I don't want Jen to have to go through any more of what's transpired the past few days to her. My informant thinks the Martino family sold Jen Davis's whereabouts to Devon Madison. If so, the man jumped at the chance to even the score with her."

"She's one tough woman who's gone through enough." Micah's hand about his cell tightened when he thought about the haunted look in Jen's eyes, as though she were shell-shocked.

"Yeah, now my question is why you didn't get the information faster about the incident in the woods on the Triple T Ranch."

"My only guess is whoever is leaking the information to the mob stalled its delivery. I'll be sending you the list of agents who had access, but it won't be narrowing it down much for you."

When Hannah finally entered Austin's hospital room an hour later, she had run the gauntlet of emotions, and yet nothing seemed to fit her for long. The one overriding feeling she couldn't shake was her love for the man lying in the bed because of her, his eyes closed, the pale cast to his skin alarming her although she knew he would be all right.

She would never have come to the ranch if she had thought she would bring killers to it. Yes, she'd always been vigilant and acknowledged the need for that, but because she was so careful she'd come to feel Devon wouldn't find her. She'd been naïve before and still was.

She intended to make sure with her own eyes that Austin would be all right, then she would leave. She wouldn't bring any more heartache to him. The night before when she'd told him the truth of who she was, that look in his eyes would stay with her forever. To him she'd betrayed what had been developing between them. And she couldn't blame him for feeling that way.

She'd never had that talk with him she'd set out to do in the middle of the night. And now it was just as well. She didn't want to bring any more pain to him or his family.

Hannah covered the width of the room and sat next to Caroline on the couch. "Where's Gil?"

"He went to get him some coffee and see his deputy before he heads back to Sweet Creek."

Maybe she could hitch a ride with him, pack her belongings and leave the ranch before Austin returned. "When will Austin be able to go home?"

"Tomorrow."

"Have you said anything to Misty?" Hannah asked while her gaze fastened onto the chiseled planes of Austin's face, relaxed now in sleep.

"No, I didn't want to tell her until I knew what was going on firsthand. I will later tonight. Austin's sister will drive us all back to the ranch after he's discharged tomorrow. If I know my grandson, he won't stay here longer than he has to. You can go back with us then, too. I'm sure my granddaughter won't mind you staying at her house tonight, either."

Hannah shook her head. "I'm going to ask Gil for a ride. I want to make sure everything at the house is cleaned up. I know Max said not to worry about it, but I don't want Misty to see anything out of place."

"Don't blame yourself, child." Caroline patted Hannah's hand lying on her thigh. "I know my grandson has deep feelings for you."

Which she destroyed last night. Her gaze strayed to Austin, still asleep in the bed. *Because of me he could have died this morning. He might forgive me. I don't forgive myself.*

A woman with beautiful green eyes and curly hair peeked into the room. "Are you Hannah? Micah McGraw called me to come talk to you." She stepped into the room, her high heels clicking against the tile floor. "I'm Violet Kramer, a reporter for the *Missoula Daily News.* I'm so glad you're all right."

"What did Mr. McGraw tell you?" Hannah remembered Austin's grandmother talking about the reporter.

"He told me about the narrow escape you had early this morning and thought I might be interested in your story. He felt a story in the paper would drive home the point of who you are to certain people in Chicago. Do you have time to talk?"

"Yes, I do." Maybe telling her story would help her decide what to do with the rest of her life. Hannah turned to Caroline and hugged the older woman. "Goodbye. I'm going to get a ride with Gil after I talk with Violet."

Hannah moved to Austin's bed and leaned down to kiss his cheek. "Goodbye, Austin. Don't hate me," she whispered close to his ear.

As she left the room, he shifted on the bed, his brow

furrowed for a few seconds, but his eyes didn't open. Seeing him with an IV attached only hammered home what she had caused.

"Thanks, Gil, for bringing me back to the ranch. Are you sure you don't mind waiting for me to pack and make sure the house is all right for the Taylors when they come back tomorrow? I'd rather stay in town this evening and take the first bus to Billings tomorrow."

Scanning the house with a path cleared to the deck, the sheriff combed his fingers through his hair. "I don't blame you with no one here tonight, especially with all that's happened to you." He looked at her. "You're a survivor, Hannah. Oh, I'm sorry. You probably want to go by Jen now."

She tilted her head and thought a moment, but every time she tried to come to a firm decision, she couldn't. "I don't know what I'm going to do. I haven't responded to that name in years. Trained myself not to. That won't be easy to undo."

"All I can say is you're one brave, gusty lady to testify against a gunrunner and put him away. A lot of people wouldn't have gotten involved."

She sent him a smile, not sure what to say to his compliment. She'd never thought of herself as either brave or gusty—just surviving from one day to the next. "I hope you'll come in while I pack."

"Sure. I'll even check the house for you, but I have to say Rene and Max are so dependable. If they say they're gonna take care of everything at the ranch, they did."

Good. She didn't want to stay any longer than necessary. That was only reinforced when she stepped through the door into the foyer. Her gaze immediately riveted to the place where the deputy had lain. Everywhere she peered a memory was ignited. She trained her attention to the small space right in front of her and marched toward her bedroom.

But the second she entered her bedroom she couldn't look away from her bed. She'd managed to hold herself together through getting the help the deputies and Austin had needed, through all the questions about what had transpired in the house, through the long ride to Missoula and the hospital, praying the whole way that Austin didn't die because of her. They hadn't talked because after he'd shot Devon and collapsed, he'd slipped in and out of consciousness. Then he'd been air-lifted to the hospital. By the time she had arrived, Austin had already gone into surgery.

But staring at the bed, she relived every second of the horror when Devon had trapped her on the bed and waved the gun in her face. The memories sent a tidal wave of emotions through her body all at once. She slid to the floor, her legs no longer able to support her. Clasping her shins, she drew herself into a ball, sobs attacking her, shredding her composure.

Why, Lord? Why did it happen to me?

No answers came, only tears. She cried for herself. She cried for Austin and what could have been if circumstances had been different. She even cried for Devon, a man so driven by hate that he'd come after her.

A rap at her door seeped into her mind. Still sitting on the floor, she jerked up and twisted about. "Yes?"

"Are you all right?" the sheriff asked. "Do you need any help?"

"No, I won't be much longer." She swiped at the

tears flowing down her face and struggled to her feet. Wobbling, she clutched the dresser close by and steadied herself.

"Okay. I'm going to the barn to talk with Max. I'll meet you out front."

Hannah moved fast, slinging clothes into her luggage, and was outside on the deck twenty minutes later after doing a walk-through so her mind would be at peace about Misty returning to a house that didn't show the violence that had occurred in it. The sheriff had been right about Max and Rene. They'd done an excellent job.

On the ride back into Sweet Creek, Gil talked nonstop about how well Max and Austin's men had taken care of the ranch and any cleanup after the house was processed. In town the sheriff dropped Hannah off at the motel not too far from the bus station. When she finally collapsed on the bed in her room, she dug into her pocket for her cell. All she wanted to do was sleep, but she still had one more thing she needed to do, something she'd put off until she was alone with plenty of time.

Punching in the number she would never forget, even after five years, she tried to compose what she would say. But the second she heard her mother's voice, she burst into tears, saying, "Mama, I've missed you so much."

"Jen? What are you doing calling? They said you couldn't." Fear sounded in her mother's voice.

Wiping her shirtsleeve across her eyes, Hannah sniffed, trying to control her crying enough to have a conversation. "Devon Madison is dead. Cullen died in prison last month. I'm free. I'm coming home." Her arms ached to hold her mother and brother. "How's Josh?"

"Okay. He's in college. This is his last year. He's

studying to be an engineer. He's..." Her mom's words came to a choking halt, her sobs renewing Hannah's.

And that was okay. There would be time later to talk. All the time in the world now.

A gust of wind swept down the street, chilling Jen as she neared Mama's Diner. The name alone produced a sweet memory of her conversation with her mother two nights ago. Yesterday she'd visited the U.S. Marshal's office and talked with Micah to straighten out all the necessary paperwork, wiping away all traces of Hannah Williams and any other version of her out there. And then she'd called Saul and arranged to see him at the hospital today.

After talking with her mom at length, she knew she had to use her birth name—Jen Davis. And after spending over a day of thinking of herself as Jen again, it hadn't been as hard as she'd thought it would be.

But every time she thought of Austin, her heart cracked even further open. She was hoping time and distance would help her heal because the hurt ran deep—a different kind of hurt from when she'd left California. She'd seen and tasted what having a real family was like. As Jen she would begin yet again a new life—one without Austin or Misty, but at least she would have her mother and brother to help. And the Lord.

Maybe one day she'd find someone who would accept Jen Davis.

For today she would have breakfast at Mama's Diner one last time before going to the hospital nearby and seeing Saul.

For the first time she entered the diner without checking the street behind her, but she couldn't stop herself from scanning the people sitting at the tables and in the booths.

Some habits would be hard to break, she thought and pulled off her gloves. She searched for Olivia but didn't see her. Had she moved on already? She'd hoped she was still here to tell her what had happened. It still felt strange for her to share openly what had occurred, but she picked up the Missoula newspaper today at the motel and saw the article Violet had written about her plight. Seeing it in black and white made it real. It was over. No more hiding. Running.

She nodded toward another waitress she knew and pointed toward where she had usually sat the month before. The young lady signaled okay and brought a cup of coffee as Jen removed her coat and took a seat.

"It looks like business as usual. How's things going since I left?" Jen flipped open the menu and decided to order something different. After all, she was a different person now.

"Good. What would you like?"

"I'll take blueberry pancakes and orange juice. Is Olivia still working here?"

The young lady shook her head. "She's been gone about three weeks or so. You're the second person asking about Olivia today."

"I am? Who else?"

The waitress pointed to a man in a booth at the front of the diner. A strikingly handsome man with blond hair sat hunched over a mug of coffee, staring at something on the table. A photo? Was that Olivia's husband?

After the young lady left, Jen stood and threaded her way through the crowd until she came to stop next to the man. He peered up at her, his eyes the bluest color—like a body of water that could go on and on.

"I'm Han—Jen Davis. I understand you've been asking about Olivia."

"Yes." He slid the photo over to her. "I'm Ford Jensen. This is a picture of my wife. Do you know her? Know where she went?"

The photo was of Olivia and the man sitting at the booth. Both were smiling, his arm slung over her shoulder. "Not exactly. I've been out of town. I knew she was moving. She was hoping to get a job working with children." She wouldn't say anything to Olivia's husband about the baby. That needed to come from Olivia. "When I knew her, she went by the name of Olivia Jarrod. Maybe that'll help you find her." Because she believed Olivia and her husband needed to talk at the very least—for their baby's sake if for nothing else.

"She didn't tell you where she was moving?"

"No, but I got the impression it was a small town."

"How is she?"

Hurting, but again she didn't think it was her place to tell him. "She was doing fine, but I always got the impression she was—sad." She started to make her way back to her table, stopped and added, "I hope you find her."

"Me, too." He dropped his head and resumed studying the photograph.

"It's good to see you. I'm so glad you called. I didn't want you to leave Billings without seeing me."

Saul's pale, battered face tore at Jen's composure. "I'm so sorry this happened to you. I never meant for anyone to get hurt."

He reached a hand toward hers on the bed next to him. "I'm the one who should apologize to you. I think I told them where to find you. My memory is still fuzzy about what exactly happened." Tears glistened in his eyes. "I'm so sorry about that."

"You have nothing to be sorry about. I never imagined anyone would find you and do that to you because of me. I…" Her own tears welled into her throat, making it difficult to speak.

"We could go on and on apologizing to each other. Let's agree to forgive and forget it. Okay?"

Nodding, she swallowed several times. "The doctor said you should make a full recovery and should be able to go home soon."

"Yeah, this body has at least another ten thousand miles on it." He attempted a smile that faded instantly. "I can't believe what happened to you at the Taylors' ranch. For that matter before. To think I know someone in the Witness Protection Program."

"Not anymore. I'm out of it now. That's why I'm going back to California tomorrow." She'd spent a half an hour the day before filling Saul in on what happened to her at Austin's, at least the part about the thugs coming after her, then she'd promised Saul she would be by to see him.

"Did you enjoy working for the Taylors? I never got around to asking you that with all you told me."

"Yes. Misty was adorable and Caroline was kind and generous." Jen sat in the chair next to his hospital bed.

"And Austin?"

"I'm alive because of him." She dropped her gaze to her lap, not wanting him to read what was probably visible in her eyes when she talked about Austin. He wouldn't let it be if he knew she loved Austin.

"Hannah," he said with a tsk and a shake of the head.

"I'm going by Jen Davis now. That's my real name. Jennifer Ann Davis." If she said it enough she would really believe it was real—not some dream that she would wake up from.

"My, that's got to be confusing. How did you keep it all straight?"

"By locking that past life out of my thoughts. I was usually successful."

"But not always?"

"No."

"Is that how you think you're gonna get over Austin when you go back to California?"

She blinked at the question. "I'm that easy to read?"

"Yep." He tapped his temple. "You can't keep much from these sharp eyes. Even when you worked for me, I could see tragedy had touched you, but I wasn't gonna pry. If you wanted to tell me, you would."

"Then why are you prying now?"

"Because Austin is a good man and he deserves someone like you to love."

"It's too late for that. I kept who I was from him. He got shot because of me. His family could have gotten caught up in it all. Thankfully they didn't but—"

"Hold it. Have you talked with Austin about this?"

"The night before the shootout at the Triple T I told him about who I was and why I was using a fake name. You should have seen the devastating look he gave me. I'll never forget it."

"Have you talked with him since then?"

She shook her head. "We were too busy fighting for our lives and then he was flown to the Missoula hospital."

"Not afterward in the hospital?"

"Well, no. It's best I move on. I've caused so much pain, even for you."

"Maybe the joy you've bought outweighs that pain. I think you need to talk to Austin after he's had some time to assimilate what you told him that night. That was a lot to take in all at once. I felt overwhelmed after your call yesterday evening."

"I don't know how he can forgive me for everything that's happened."

"There's only one way to find out. Ask him." Saul's sharp gaze assessed her. "Or are you so used to denying yourself that it's easier to run away than face Austin one last time?"

Later that evening as she laid out what she was going to wear on her trip the next day to California, she couldn't get Saul's question out of her mind. Was that what she was doing? Was she running away? She'd become quite good at that.

As hard as it was, she thought back to what Devon had done to her. She had to forgive him because he'd ruled her every action for five long years and she didn't want him to for another second. She had to let go totally if she was going to be truly free. If the Lord could forgive her sins, then she could Devon and Cullen. She'd started the process back in the hospital chapel. Now she completed it. The thought of letting go of the past, like a prisoner being released from captivity, lifted a burden from her. Peace settled all around her. The taste of freedom made her want so much more.

Maybe she could fly to California and get reacquainted with her mother and brother. Then after some time, she could come back to Montana and Austin would at least see her, give her a chance to tell him how much she loved him and was so sorry for everything that had happened.

Maybe he would forgive her.

A knock at the door interrupted her thoughts.

When she checked the peephole, her heartbeat began to race.

Austin.

How did he find— Saul. She should have figured Saul would call Austin.

With her hand on the knob, she slowly turned it. She'd left without a word except a note that she had hastily scribbled on a pad in his office right before she'd left that last time. She said she didn't need the money owed her.

That's it. That's why he's here. It's about the back wages.

When the door swung open to reveal him, Jen sucked in a deep breath and held it. He looked wonderful to her, and yet the past week had taken a toll on him. He sported a sling and she imagined under his coat and shirt a bandaged shoulder. But the worst was the look in his eyes, as though he hadn't slept in days. Maybe he hadn't with all that had to be done at the ranch.

He waved a piece of paper in her face, anger slashing his features. "Is this your way of saying goodbye? I don't want your money. I want you."

Her eyes widened. "What did you say?"

"I had at least expected you to be at the ranch even if you didn't stay at the hospital." He moved past her into the room. "We have unfinished business." He pivoted toward her. "And it isn't going to be done long distance or with a note."

Anger still poured off him, but its edges softened as his gaze skimmed over her, taking all of her in. She wanted to melt into his arms, but she held herself taut, a few feet from him. "After all that happened I didn't think you'd want to see me. You could have been killed because of me."

He took a step toward her. "And you could have been killed because of me. Remember the fire in the barn."

"But the night before when I told you who I really was you were so mad at me."

"I was in shock. Trying to process what you'd told me. And, yes, I was angry at first. I love you and wanted you to trust me."

"I did. I'd never told a soul who I was. That was a big step for me."

"Yeah, I know. I figured that out in the middle of another sleepless night. I'd planned to talk to you about it then everything blew up in our faces." He quirked one corner of his mouth, no anger visible now in his face.

She took a step toward him. Inches separated them. Peering up at him, she kept her arms at her side. "I haven't gotten a chance to thank you for saving my life yet again."

"I still love you." He wrapped her in his embrace. "We could keep a running tally of who saved who, but personally I'm hoping we live to a ripe old age together with no more near-death experiences. In the past month I've had enough excitement to last me a lifetime."

"Live together?"

His grin broadened. "That's my roundabout way of asking you to marry me, Jen Davis. Will you?"

She nuzzled closer, conscious of his injured shoulder. "Yes! Yes! I can't think of anything more perfect than marrying the man I love."

"It's about time you said it." He lowered his mouth and claimed hers in a deep kiss that sealed their future.

* * * * *

Dear Reader,

I had so much fun with this book. Being a part of a group of authors who write connecting stories is a challenge—a big puzzle that I need to solve. I love working puzzles, and that's what appeals to me when I write a continuity story. There is a lot of work involved, making sure the books are linked seamlessly. I hope you enjoyed the third installment in this Love Inspired Suspense continuity series.

I love hearing from readers. You can contact me at margaretdaley@gmail.com or at P.O. Box 2074, Tulsa, OK 74101. You can also learn more about my books at www.margaretdaley.com. I have a quarterly newsletter that you can sign up for on my Web site or you can enter my monthly drawings by signing my guest book on the Web site.

Best wishes,

Margaret Daley

QUESTIONS FOR DISCUSSION

1. Trust is important in a relationship. Austin was scared to trust after what his deceased wife did. Hannah didn't know who to trust. Has anyone caused you to distrust him/her? Why? How did you settle it?

2. Who is your favorite character? Why?

3. Have you ever been really scared? How did you deal with it?

4. Hannah didn't think the Lord answered her prayers. Have you ever thought that? What did you do?

5. What is your favorite scene? Why?

6. What would you have done if you had been in Hannah's shoes and witnessed a murder?

7. Hannah didn't have a lot of hope for having a family, so while she was at the ranch, she visualized Austin, Caroline and Misty as her family, if only for a short time. How important is your family to you? What are some special things you do with your family?

8. Hannah testified in a trial to put a killer in prison. That took courage. What have you done that required courage? Did any Scriptures help you through it? What are they?

9. Misty nearly died in a car wreck. This was hard for

Austin to handle. When life seems impossible, what do you do? Who do you turn to for help?

10. Hannah fell in love when she tried not to because she knew there wasn't a future for her and Austin. Have you ever done something against your better judgment? How did it turn out?

11. What does "God is my refuge and strength" mean to you?

12. Have you ever kept a secret that if it came out it would harm either you or someone else? Did it come out? What happened?

13. Why did Hannah's faith waver since she was in the Witness Protection Program? What could she have done differently?

14. Hannah enjoyed living in the small Montana town, while Austin's wife had longed for the city. Which do you prefer, city or country? Why?

15. Dealing with an injured child is a difficult situation for a parent to go through. How would you have responded if you were Austin?

Olivia Jarrod thought testifying against
Vincent Martino was the right thing to do,
but now pregnant and with a price on her head,
she's no longer sure.
Read on for a preview of DEADLY VOWS
by Shirlee McCoy,
the next exciting book in the
PROTECTING THE WITNESSES *series.*

She'd popped.

Olivia Jarrod turned sideways and stared at her reflection, not sure if she should be elated or horrified. The flat plane of her stomach was gone. In its place was a subtle roundness. She placed her hands on the bump, imagining tiny hands and feet.

Her baby.

And Ford's.

She frowned. Thinking about Ford was something she tried not to do. The past few months had been difficult enough without reliving her failed marriage, thinking about the year they had been separated or dwelling on the last time she'd seen him.

She still didn't know why he'd shown up on the doorstep of her bungalow a few days after Christmas. Had he been lonely in their penthouse? Had he decided to fight for their marriage?

Olivia had asked herself those questions over and over again in the days after she'd fled, but she had no answers. All she knew was that Ford didn't want kids.

He'd be shocked if he found out she was pregnant.

Appalled.

Angry.

It was a good thing she knew it. Otherwise, she'd do what she knew she wasn't supposed to do. She'd call Ford. She'd tell him that he was going to be a father.

And she'd probably end up dying because of it.

After all, wasn't that the first rule of witness protection?

No contact with anyone or anything from the past.

People who followed the rule lived. People who didn't died.

To read more of Olivia and Ford's story,
pick up DEADLY VOWS
by Shirlee McCoy,
available in April
from Love Inspired Suspense.

Love Inspired
A Mother's Gift
Arlene James
Kathryn Springer
Two Stories of
Mother's Day
Blessings

Love Inspired®
SUSPENSE

TITLES AVAILABLE NEXT MONTH

Available April 13, 2010

ON THIN ICE
Whisper Lake
Linda Hall

DEADLY VOWS
Protecting the Witnesses
Shirlee McCoy

CALCULATED REVENGE
Jill Elizabeth Nelson

MOUNTAIN PERIL
Sandra Robbins

LISCNMBPA0310

With each stride that brought the cowboy closer, her heart increased its pounding.

She took a step back.

Nearing her, he smiled, but all she could focus on was the cleft in his chin and another man she knew with one. The sight of it instantly threw her back into the past....

Devon Madison brushed up against her as she left the courthouse. The hatred spewing from him held her immobile. He leaned close and whispered, "I'm coming after you."

She forced the memory back.

"Are you Hannah Williams?"

The question from the cowboy in front of her whisked her totally back to the present. *No, I'm Jen Davis.* But not anymore. "Yes."

PROTECTING THE WITNESSES:

New identities, looming danger and forever love in the Witness Protection Program.

Twin Targets–Marta Perry, January 2010
Killer Headline–Debby Giusti, February 2010
Cowboy Protector–Margaret Daley, March 2010
Deadly Vows–Shirlee McCoy, April 2010
Fatal Secrets–Barbara Phinney, May 2010
Risky Reunion–Lenora Worth, June 2010

Books by Margaret Daley

Love Inspired Suspense

Hearts on the Line
Heart of the Amazon
So Dark the Night
Vanished
Buried Secrets
Don't Look Back
Forsaken Canyon
What Sarah Saw
Poisoned Secrets
Cowboy Protector

Love Inspired

**A Mother for Cindy*
**Light in the Storm*
The Cinderella Plan
**When Dreams Come True*
**Tidings of Joy*
***Once Upon a Family*
***Heart of the Family*
***Family Ever After*
A Texas Thanksgiving
Second Chance Family

*The Ladies of Sweetwater Lake
**Fostered by Love

MARGARET DALEY

feels she has been blessed. She has been married more than thirty years to her husband, Mike, whom she met in college. He is a terrific support and her best friend. They have one son, Shaun. Margaret has been writing for many years and loves to tell a story. When she was a little girl, she would play with her dolls and make up stories about their lives. Now she writes these stories down. She especially enjoys weaving stories about families and how faith in God can sustain a person when things get tough. When she isn't writing, she is fortunate to be a teacher for students with special needs. Margaret has taught for more than twenty years and loves working with her students. She has also been a Special Olympics coach and has participated in many sports with her students.